BITTER LIGHT

Clara Grigorescu

BITTER LIGHT

Copyright © 2016 Aquanti Media, LLC

ISBN: 069279462X
ISBN-13: 978-0692794623 (Aquanti Media, LLC)

Library of Congress Control Number: 2016917631
Aquanti Media, LLC, Bellevue, WASHINGTON

Printed in the United States of America
10 9 8 7 6 5 4 3 2 1

Book design by Cristian Grigorescu

This is partial work of fiction. Names, characters and incidents are the product of the author's imagination or are used fictitiously. The places and historical events are true.

IN LOVING MEMORY

Clara Grigorescu
March 10th, 1973 – June 25th, 2016

Fifteen thousand mornings, give or take, is all she got. Most of us get twice as many.

My sister Clara was born to be something special. She will live forever in the hearts of those she touched. Today is my chance to say *thank you* for the way my sister has brightened my life. To honor her existence, I have decided to publish her work. This book, an adaptation based on a love-story screenplay she wrote in 2008, is dedicated to all of our family and friends.

Georgia Clara was born on March 10, 1973, in Constanta, Romania. We used to call her by her middle name, Clara, or Clari. From early childhood my sister was drawn to art. She was the most creative person I've ever known. She admired fashion, design, and all forms of art-making. She loved to paint and to craft beautiful things by hand, and we are blessed to have those pieces now that she is gone. She was extremely romantic, which is reflected in *Bitter Light*, her screenplay. She was a true artist but she never considered herself a writer. *Bitter Light* represents the only screenplay she has ever written. She was fascinated with this story.

We grew up in the 1980s in Communist Romania. It was an arduous childhood, but when I look back, I wouldn't change a thing. It was full of wonderful memories. Maybe that childhood made us unbreakable and united us even more. It prepared us for what was to come. As children, I was her best toy. Both of our parents were busy with their careers, and, only six years older than me, she raised me like no one else could have. She held my hand when I was small, she caught me when I fell, and she continued to do so until the last moments of her life. My sister will always be my hero. Her beauty was so pure. Her smile constantly lit up a room, and those eyes, those beautiful eyes, will never be forgotten.

Above all, she was so beautiful with kindness.

The two of us immigrated to the United States in 1996. She was twenty-three at the time, and I was only a teenager. After spending the first two years in New Orleans, we moved to Seattle, where my sister would spend the remainder of her short life. Moving away from home, immigrating to a foreign place, made our love and passion for each other grow immensely. She was magical; she carved the future for me in the way she knew best. Her life was full of dreams and imagination. She always believed she was here for a reason. She was the kindest person I'll ever know: always one to forgive first and to put others before her.

Clara spent most of her career working in the medical field. She was an esthetician, employed for over a decade in a dermatology office in Bellevue, Washington. She also worked in cosmetics as a beauty advisor for Lancome and as a regional manager at Victoria's Secret. When she wasn't working, she enjoyed life with family and friends. She didn't travel much; she detested flying. Anytime she would travel, she would only go on road trips.

The nightmare settled upon us on November 19, 2014, when we found out she was diagnosed with stage IV non-small cell adenocarcinoma lung cancer. The original prognosis, which she chose not to disclose to our whole family including me, in attempt to protect us, was that she had only nine months to live. It was devastating enough for those close to her—her closest friends and family—just knowing about the advanced lung cancer. This type of disease, for a non-smoker, was extremely rare.

The initial treatment was chemotherapy, of which she received only two treatments because the DNA results revealed that she had a genetic mutation, which qualified her for a targeted therapy treatment. Therefore, after that initial systemic chemotherapy treatment, she was placed on a newer oral chemotherapeutic drug assimilated once a day, which in turn would be easier on the body. She continued to have a normal life, as the symptoms were minimal. But in May 2015, after a routine checkup, the CT scan showed progression of the cancer, which meant that her cancer had mutated and was no longer responding to the medication. This was a major disappointment to everyone, especially Clara, but she kept focused and continued to have a positive outlook. After several procedures and biopsies, the doctors determined that there was another treatment option against the new mutation. It was also a targeted therapy, an oral chemotherapeutic drug to be taken daily. This was great news, but there was a trick; this agent was only available through clinical trials.

To get my sister on the trial took months. During the summer of 2015, while waiting to get approved for the trial, she decided to get another dose of chemotherapy, but the response was nonexistent. At this point, chemotherapy was off the table. Her opponent was strong and tricky.

In the fall of 2015, the medication that we so desperately were waiting for was finally approved by the FDA, and she immediately started to take it. We saw a big improvement over the next few months. By Christmas of 2015, we were all hoping she would go into remission, for she showed almost no symptoms. But we were all blind to the storm that was about to come. Toward the end of February 2016, she began coughing again. A chest X-ray and a CT scan showed inflamed lymph nodes and a tumor that was pressing on the bronchioles as well as on the artery, almost completely occluding it. Clara underwent full chest radiation in the hopes that the tumor would shrink and the symptoms would improve. In an incredible paradox, she made the pain look beautiful; she wore that smile in a situation where anyone else would cry. She looked and behaved as though nothing was wrong even though the pain from the radiation was so severe that she was unable to drink fluids or eat solid foods. She did the best she could at that moment; she still fought and believed that she would beat the monster.

Then, in early May, Clara was diagnosed with leptomeningeal carcinomatosis. Leptomeningeal carcinomatosis (LC) is a rare complication of cancer in which the disease spreads to the membranes (meninges) surrounding the brain and spinal cord. Once again, her opponent was striking back with a vengeance. She was given four to eight weeks to live. Even at that point, we didn't lose hope; we kept trying to find other treatments in the United States as well as around the world. I was desperate to find a treatment that could prolong her life. For her part, although she was carrying the world on her shoulders, she never complained. The rest of us cried more than she ever did. I will never know what was going through her mind, how she felt in realizing that the present moment was the only thing she had.

What would you do if you knew you had only a few weeks left to live? I know what she did. She kept on smiling and pretending nothing was wrong. She gave us time, probably the most important gift of all. All she wanted was to live, to live a little longer for her family and friends. She couldn't bear to see us hurt. She was extremely strong, very ambitious, and not afraid of treatments. She was a true fighter. Clari was just herself and the world loved her for it. She used to say, "When the time comes, when the time comes," but indeed she always believed she would be cured. In reality, though, she never had a second chance.

Clara was only forty-three when she succumbed on June 25, 2016, after a year-and-a-half-long battle with lung cancer. She died in Bellevue, Washington, surrounded by family and friends, who had given her the strength to smile and to stay positive throughout the fight.

Even though it was short, Clara's life was full—filled with adventures, romance, and love. Her multiple marriages gave her a full life even though she had no children. Regardless if God only granted her half of a normal lifespan, it was enough to become a beacon of inspiration for all of us who knew her. She touched so many lives in a positive way. We will always, always feel cheated that she was taken from us so young.

I've been thinking of the flat line on a hospital-room monitor as being a horizon line, which she crossed while holding my hand. As difficult as this change in my life is, I know I will endure the pain, remembering this.

In the end, this book is just another way for me to express my gratitude for everything she has ever done for me, our family, and her friends. There will never be another woman like Clara, whose beauty both internal and external will never be extinguished from the minds of those who knew her.

When we look up, we know she's smiling down on us. Maybe she's somewhere among those young stars in the night sky. She is home now, and I know she's watching over her loved ones until we all meet again.

— Cristian Grigorescu

CONTENTS

ACKNOWLEDGMENTS

There are many people who have helped me with this project but none more than my family: Ana, Massimo, and my mother, Maria. I thank them for their support and encouragement.

I am very grateful to my brilliant editor and co-writer, Cara Diaconoff. My thanks also to my sisters' friends, Daniela Murray, Tanya Melnik, David Mordekhov and Mircea Goia, who provided a spark of inspiration.

I would also like to thank my sister's friend from early childhood who has helped her with the original screenplay. She decided to remain anonymous in this publication.

Huge thanks also to my friends Deepak Mani and Anne Baker who consulted with me throughout this project.

Finally, I thank the people of Constanta, whose suffering and endurance under the Communist regime have impelled my sister and her friends to tell their story.

THE ICON

The streets were almost deserted on this gloomy afternoon, the temperature just shy of freezing. Old maples and oaks lined the roads in icy splendor. It was the time of year when families were gathered around the fireplace.

A cab rolled through the cold, slick streets, carrying two men, father and son, to a Christmas party in Bedford, New York. The two rode in silence, the truce that normally obtained between them being too easily broken by words. They faced away from each other, each looking out his window, admiring the scenery.

The houses in this part of town were tall, built a century before, and sparkling now with holiday decorations. The front windows and porticos of the handsome homes shone with lamplight, and the world seemed at peace. As they drove further into the neighborhood, the homes got even larger, each with a long private driveway.

David, the son, sat in the taxi smoking a cigarette. He raised it to his lips with hands that more than one woman had commented were "beautifully masculine." He'd never been sure what that meant, but he sometimes found it amusing to ponder. David was a man in his late thirties, tall and well-built with black hair clipped very short. Alex, his father, was a polished man in his early sixties, still good-looking, with a full head of salt-and-pepper hair. David lived in New York; Alex was visiting him for the holidays from his own home in Southern California.

Winter had always been David's favorite season. Most people thought of the cold as harsh, but for him there was something about cold weather that softened everyone, including himself. And, of course, he always thought about *her* at Christmas, although it had been so long since they had last seen each other.

That was about to change, he guessed. He was not sure if she would be at the party, but given that she was the lady of the house, it would be surprising if she were not. His life could usually be relied upon to present impossibly ironic situations, and he supposed the joke was once again on him.

They arrived at Phillip's mansion, which was built in seventeenth-century French Chateau style with heavy masonry façade and large windows, topped with steep roof ridges and massive chimneys. They rolled through the front gates and slowly up the large circular driveway edged with English boxwoods shrubs.

"Not all of us can be so lucky," said the driver, admiringly.

"Indeed!" responded David.

Phillip was David's boss, the publisher at the monthly magazine where David had recently begun working as an editor.

The two disembarked from the cab. Alex took a little longer to do so; David, extinguishing his cigarette under his foot, was already admiring the front of the property.

"Dad, check out this amazing place."

"Imagine how beautiful summers are here," Alex replied, staring at a frozen water fountain. He spoke with a slight Eastern-European accent.

The gravel underneath their feet sounded crisply as they walked to the front steps. Their knock on the door was answered almost at once by a houseboy, who showed them into a lavish foyer and took their coats. David blew on his hands to warm them up.

Phillip greeted them in short order. Phillip was in his early fifties, stocky-figured, sure of himself—not necessarily good-looking but possessed of an edgy charisma. Jazz music and a muffled din sounded from the living room behind him.

"You finally made it," he boomed. "That eighteen-year old bottle of single malt is waiting."

"You have no idea how much I need that," replied David. "It's pretty cold out there."

"I haven't opened it yet," remarked Phillip. "I was saving it for you." He was looking at Alex expectantly.

"This is my father, Alex," said David.

Alex and Phillip shook hands.

"What a beautiful house you've got, Phillip," said Alex. "It's a pleasure to meet you."

"Nice meeting you, Alex," said Phillip. "I hope this weather isn't too cold for you Californians."

"I'll survive," Alex answered wryly.

"Come on in and make yourself comfortable. I was *so* looking forward to meet you. I've heard so much about you and your adventures." With that, Philip turned and disappeared down the hallway toward the party, not looking behind to see if they were following.

They had lingered to admire the large, airy interior,

full of antiques and old paintings. Everything exuded wealth worn graciously. The marble floors shone pristinely. The aroma of expensive cigars wafted through the house.

"This is well put together," said Alex. "He has good taste—or a good interior decorator."

"Oh, he's a patented slob," said David. "You should see his office."

"He seems a nice enough guy to work for."

"Haven't really been there long enough to know one way or another," rejoined David, a little testily.

"I thought you'd been there two months by now," said Alex.

David said nothing to this.

They moved into the living room and stood on the edge of the crowd. This consisted so far of sixteen or twenty people who seemed polished in a new-money way—flashy, dyed-blond, pastel-colored clothing—that contrasted with the old-fashioned elegance of the house. It was a contrast typical enough of Phillip, David reflected cynically. Phillip had made a bundle of money in real estate and only recently entered the publishing world.

"Would you like a drink, Dad?" asked David.

"Not right now," said Alex. "Thanks anyway."

"Well, I suppose I'll go take Phillip up on his offer," said David.

The living room featured ceiling-high windows on one side that overlooked the bay at the bottom of a steep hill. Alex went to one of these to take in the view.

David, meanwhile, having failed to find Phillip but having obtained a glass of wine from a waiter, wandered through another hallway looking at the art. He saw a small room with the door ajar. It looked like a woman's study—and cluttered, unlike the rest of the house. There were paintings on the floor leaning against the walls, a rolled-up exercise machine, a profusion of books and papers, a couple of overflowing boxes in a corner, and a scratched old desk by the window. There was also a Regency green velvet sofa in need of new upholstery.

David took a sip of his wine and stepped into the room. The hardwood floor creaked beneath his feet. He wasn't sure what he was looking for, but it had occurred to him this room might be *hers*, even before his eye was caught by an old wooden painted icon on the desk.

Could it be--?

He moved closer to it. Stunned, he reached out to touch its frame. His hand was trembling.

Just then, Phillip passed by in the hallway.

"Here you are!" he cried. "Santa Baby," he sang in an off-key voice. "What are you doing? I was looking for you." He came up to peer over David's shoulder at the icon.

David turned around, hand still on the object. "This is a beautiful Ioannes Korais."

"Really interesting, huh!" said Phillip. "I don't know too much about it, but you should ask my Emma. She picks out everything. This is her home office." He paused. "Ioannes Korais . . . . How the hell would you know that? The guy's pretty obscure."

David turned to look at Phillip and then back at the icon. "I saw something just like it in the past," he murmured. "It might even have been this very piece."

"You don't say," said Phillip. "Good reason to have a drink of that scotch, no?" He held out a freshly poured glass of scotch and swapped it with David's glass of wine.

David smiled. "It's a great reason to have a drink." Under his breath, he added, "I do try to drown my demons in whiskey, but I always find out the little suckers can swim." He let Phillip lead him back to the party.

THE GAME OF LIFE

It was getting darker outside, and many more people had arrived. Across the living room by one of the big windows, Alex was deep in conversation with a man who looked his own age. Alex, sensing David's gaze, stopped and sent his son a questioning glance. David caught his father's eye and nodded, signaling he was all right. Alex returned to his conversation.

David's gaze moved from one partygoer to another. He heard bits of conversation. He knew many of these people slightly, from work at the magazine. But he felt strange, disconnected. His eyes scanned the crowd. He told himself he wasn't searching for her. His gaze passed over an older woman, a younger woman, someone's chewing mouth, a woman's décolletage, a couple touching knees, and a woman in a red dress talking to a small group. Recognizing her vaguely, he moved in her direction.

She was talking in a loud voice, perhaps already drunk or maybe just exuberant; he didn't know her well enough to say. "I'm so tired of advertisers telling me how to do my job!" she declared.

"Let's not talk about work tonight," a man near her was saying. "Who's done anything fun lately?"

"Hey, I have," said the woman in red. "I've just done Vegas. Lost money with pleasure!"

"You don't seem like someone who'd misplace her pleasure for too long," said the man with a passive-aggressive smile. The woman threw him a brief sneer.

"I 'fess up to my addictions," she said. "But you know, I do always seem to find love in Vegas—and this new resort Bellagio was amazing. We were there at the opening last year."

"You always find love in Vegas?" said the man. "Doesn't seem to last you too long."

"It only needs to be long enough to recharge my batteries," rejoined the woman in a mock-flirtatious tone.

"Whatever you say, sweetheart."

"I haven't been to Vegas in ten years," blurted David.

He stared into his glass. Drunkenness could sometimes bridge a state of invisibility to one of unconsciousness, for him. He guessed it didn't quite do it this time.

— DAVID —
WEDNESDAY, NOVEMBER 29, 1989

Ten years earlier, David had been in Las Vegas at The Mirage hotel lounge in the wee hours of the morning, just him and the bartender. It had been drawing on to winter then, as well. He'd been leaning lazily on the bar.

"So," said the bartender, "what brings you here to Vegas, business or pleasure?" He had a heavy Eastern European accent and was a little older than David, tall and good-looking in a rough sort of way.

"Just trying to enjoy a piece of civilization while I still can," drawled David. "I'm flying out in the morning to uncharted territory."

In truth, he could have flown out from Los Angeles, his home. But he was recovering from a recent divorce, and he'd been trying to spend as little time as he could at home in the wake of it. He'd come to Vegas to do an interview for an article he was working on and had arranged a departure flight to Europe from there.

"If you call this civilization," said the bartender.

"Oh yeah? What do you mean?"

"Well, I immigrated from Bulgaria years ago, thinking Vegas was the place for me. But I realized that people are so depressed here. They drink themselves to death after losing so much money to capitalism. I've never seen so many drunk women in my life as I did the first week this hotel was open."

"Ohhh, you're getting too political for me, pal!" said David with a grin.

"I mean, most people coming here're looking to get *away* from civilization," said the bartender. "If that's your plan, then this is your place." He kept wiping the bar.

David looked around the empty, cavernous room, with its Formica chairs and crepe banners hanging from the walls. He took a sip of his drink and turned back to the bartender. "Doesn't get any better than this."

"You must be headed for a real shithole, to say that," observed the bartender. "Here's a drink on the house." He poured some Jack Daniel's whiskey into a glass and slid it across.

"Actually, I don't know," said David. He picked up the glass and downed the liquid in one swallow. "Could be the land of Xanadu, could be the land of the Golden Outhouse."

"Why're you going then?" queried the bartender.

"Because I'm always curious." David took a deep drag of his cigarette and exhaled forcefully. He leaned his head on his hand and focused, cross-eyed, on the cigarette ember. "And also, my old man is there—again. For years he's been doing this, going back and forth, chasing old demons or who knows what." He paused. "I find out he's in the hospital. His heart is giving him trouble, but he's so tough, he didn't even tell me. I had to find out from his insurance company. That just pissed me off. I get a phone call my father is in some godforsaken country, in some godforsaken hospital, and hey, could I confirm with the Embassy myself. I went *whoa* . . . what the hell is going on. So I call my mother and sure enough, she freaks out. 'Sweetie, that's exactly why I left the son of a bitch.' And then she starts in with her tales about foreign hospitals and weird experiments, and my hair is standing on end, so I finally book the trip, and I even lie about what I do to get a fucking visa to get there."

"Why did you have to lie?"

"Reporters aren't granted entry visas to Communist countries so easily," explained David.

"Ah, the Soviet bloc," said the bartender. "Like I said, I know something about that part of the world. It's not so terrible. Lots of booze and lots of beautiful women. The women are just incredible." He drew the shape of a curvy woman with his hands in the air and laughed knowingly. "I'll bet your dad's been having a grand old time."

"Ha, that's possible," said David. He hesitated. "He

doesn't know I'm coming. I didn't tell him. We had a big falling-out some time back. We can't have the simplest fucking conversation without getting on each other's nerves. He thinks I've got no idea what's going on, that I'm somehow oblivious to my surroundings. He told me I didn't know how to want things in life. Whatever, some crazy Eastern European idea. What's there to know how to want?"

"I'm with you there," said the bartender. "My old man has always given me shit. I like working in the bar—even if the customers are depressed. Chicks and all . . . . I like my life, man. He thinks my life is crap and my job isn't manly enough. Like I should have to work in a factory like he did all his life."

David appeared not to have heard. "There was nothing in my life that I really wanted badly," he said.

"Man," said the bartender, "you are messed up. That makes for a pretty boring life."

"I love your spirit," said David drily.

———

Back at the party, the woman in red was still talking.

"Turns out I got married in Vegas," she said. She swiveled toward David suddenly. "Hey! David, right? Are you with us?"

David returned her stare. "Yeah," he said.

"For a moment there you looked lost."

"I wasn't," said David.

"I actually got married in Vegas," the woman said again, returning to the group.

"Did you win or did you lose?" asked David.

She laughed. "I don't know yet."

Phillip came up to the group. "You guys sound like you're having fun. Winning, losing—are you playing a game?"

"Yeah, Phillip," said David. "There's always a game to be played in life. Life itself is a game. You should know . . . you seem pretty good at it."

"The game of life, huh?" said Phillip. He seemed to ignore David's sarcastic tone. Indeed, he and David had never developed a rapport, to put it mildly, and he could give back the sarcasm as good as he got. "You're right, David. That's my favorite game." He paused, smiled. "Are you playing it straight or jagged?"

"Jagged?" said one of the men in the group. "What do you mean?"

"When you play by the rules you're playing it straight," said David. "When you make your own rules, you're jagged."

"Or in other words, cheating," said the woman in red. She turned conspiratorially to the woman next to her. "I already like this game. I'm pretty jagged myself."

"Cheating is really part of this particular game," said David.

"Let's play," said Phillip. "How does it work? Who makes the rules?"

"Ah, the game of life," said Alex, who had just joined the group.

They arranged themselves around the fireplace, David facing the grate.

"Each of us has one ace," said David. "You tell a story about your life that shows you using your ace. You are the only one who can give your ace the power to win the game. Only if the story that you tell shows you're strong enough, can you keep it and make it a winner. When you win a round, you get to call the shots. If you lose, you're out."

"So what are the aces?" asked Phillip.

"Whatever gives you depth, strength, or power," said David.

"Okay, Alex," said Phillip, "you go first. Show us your ace."

Alex waited a beat. "Desire," he said. "My ace is desire."

Phillip and Alex exchanged a look.

"Go on," said Phillip.

Alex looked pensive. "I remember this one time when I was a child . . . ."

CONSTANTA

Constanta, Romania. It was late spring—the war had just ended, and the port was bustling. Little Alexander, a seven-year-old ragamuffin, was roaming the busy, dusty streets by the harbor.

There were Russian troops everywhere, walking the streets and getting drunk with the locals in the taverns by the harbor. Romanian flags waved in the breeze alongside Soviet flags on almost every balcony. The Soviets were the liberators from the Nazis, and they proudly flew their hammer and sickle everywhere.

Alex ran up the hill toward a residential neighborhood. He went through a tall iron gate with two lions on each side into an overgrown front garden. The house looked like it had once been imposing but had now grown tired, in need of remodeling.

On the unkempt lawn, children—better dressed than Alex, in pleated pants and linen shirts—were playing, and adults were lounging. There were cups of tea and plates of petit-fours on a rough-hewn table set with lace doilies. Two men and two women sat listening to the news on a radio.

"That's it, we're doing it," said one of the men. "We're going to America."

"Are you going to sell everything?" asked the other man. He was the owner of the house to which this garden belonged.

"I already sold everything," said the first man, laughing bitterly. "The Russians are here, and my friend, they are here to stay. So we're going. We're here only because our oldest is still recovering from scarlet fever. As soon as he's better, we're leaving."

One of the two women drinking tea was tall and thin; the other was fuller and more vulgar, dressed in lavish but tasteless new clothes. The tall, thin woman noticed Alex with a smile.

"He's the boy we'll take with us when we're leaving," said the other woman. "His parents died during the war in a bombardment." She motioned toward her husband, the man who had spoken of leaving soon for America. "He promised them we'll look after him."

Alex ran up to her, but with a jerky motion, she shoved him away. He stood stunned for a second and then ran on. He missed his parents and tacitly accepted the idea that no one else would love him as they had. He had already grown used to being alone and rejected.

Outside the servants' entrance, he saw a brand-new black Ford Coupe. He had never seen a big American make, and to him, the car seemed from a different universe. It had recently been cleaned and its paint buffed and polished to perfection. The white rims and shiny black paint gleamed in the sunlight.

Alex stopped, fascinated. Slowly he advanced toward the car. He reached toward it but didn't dare touch it.

Everything about the car was big and luxurious. Alex walked all around it, touched the chrome front bumper, gazed inside its windows, and put his cheek against the door. He wanted the car to be his. He knew it was impossible. He was just a rumpled little kid in love with a wonder of engineering.

"I thought only gods could have something so beautiful," said Alex now. "I was afraid that if I touched it, the car would simply disappear. That night I learned to desire."

Desire, thought David, was a fancier word than *need,* but how his father loved it. It was what got him out of bed in the morning. He worked to fulfill his *desires.* He never called them his *dreams* or his *goals.* It was always his *desires.* It had become a life lesson David had learned since his early childhood.

David knew about Alex's hard childhood—granted, more from his own conjectures and from stray bits of information his mother had told him than from Alex himself. His father had always insisted it was useless to dwell on the painful things in life; even the story he had just told had ended on that image of the gorgeous car. He hadn't gone into detail about the awful adoptive parents, but David knew some of that story. David's adoptive grandmother, the vulgar lady in the skintight clothes, had treated young Alex like a poor relation at best. The family had moved to Southern California; the father had within a few short years become a well-off builder. Tuition at private high schools and college had been paid for the natural children, but Alex had had to put himself through the state university, working as a supermarket cashier. Jobs in the family business had been reserved for the natural children, while Alex had had to fend for himself. It was tough, but he never stopped dreaming, never stopped thinking of his "desires."

He began to fulfill them. After college he had gotten hired at an office-supply manufacturer and learned the business; by forty, he had opened his own company, which now had branches all over the region and competed well against the big chains.

As far as David knew, his father had nothing any longer to do with his adoptive family. Alex had met David's mother, Rita, when she was hired as a secretary in his company, a job she had quit as soon as they were married, in line with societal expectations for women at that time but also in line with his mother's own . . . *desires*. David's mother wasn't really interested in working for a living; she was a romantic type who had been drawn to both the physique and the idea of a dashing Romanian. Among the many ways his father had disappointed her was in his refusal to talk about Romania. He associated the place with failure and desperation; the only Romanians he'd really known were his adoptive family, who had been cruel and coarse. He had made it a point to avoid building connections with fellow Romanians in Los Angeles.

That was why it had been such a shock to David, around the time he graduated from college, when Alex began to book trips back to the old country. Alex had sold his shares in his company by then; he was semi-retired.

The first trip had taken place shortly after David's mother and father had been divorced; Alex had been gone for weeks, close to a whole summer. All David knew, from his mother, was that Alex had gone "to Romania"—he didn't know where in the country that meant or whom, if anyone, Alex was visiting there. As far as David had known, Alex no longer knew a soul in that country.

Maybe it was nostalgia. Or maybe he was in search of something. Who knew why a man would return to a country he hadn't seen in decades?

David's mother, for her part, seemed angry that it was one more thing Alex had kept back from her. There was so much he had never wanted to share with her. It was as if she was just a prop in his life, she would complain: a cardboard cutout with the label Wife.

David had to admit he knew the feeling.

David had always appreciated his father most from a distance—like earlier that night, at the party, when father and son had caught each other's eye across the room and Alex had sent him that questioning look, making sure he didn't need anything, making sure he was all right. It was at moments like that, that he appreciated his father's reserve, his subtlety.

Up close, however, it was a different matter. Alex could be abrupt, severe; for all his talk of *desires*, he would not brook everyday talk about emotions.

— **DAVID** —
LOS ANGELES, 1987

The falling-out they had had—the one David had mentioned to the Vegas bartender—had come about over the topic of the Romanian trips. Alex had just returned from his second one of them, which had taken place less than a year after the first. Father and son had met for dinner in L.A. at one of the dimly lit, muted steakhouses Alex had always favored. He had been characteristically quiet on the subject of his trip, murmuring a few platitudes about the crumbling grandeur of the buildings and the untapped potential of the people. At least David knew this time that Alex had been to Constanta, his old hometown.

"How much of it did you remember?" asked David, digging for details.

Alex had demurred with a wave of his hand. "Oh . . . at seven years old, what does one take in to remember?

"What about you?" he had gone on, trying to change the subject. "How goes the life of the young stringer?"

David hated it when his father adopted that patronizing tone. His father barely seemed to know what he did for a living; David wasn't, in fact, a stringer but had a steady, although of course ill-paid, job as a reporter at a small suburban daily. It was his first job out of college, and he'd been in it nine months. He was itching to get out.

"Fine, Dad," he'd said. He let a moment go by while he swallowed a bite of potato. "You know," he said, "the next time you go to Romania—I assume there'll be a next time before long—why couldn't I come with you? I could quit my job and file freelance articles—really *be* a stringer, you know. It's the way a lot of important writers get started. Go to where a story might be: find a story that isn't the obvious one. I mean, look at how that part of the world is opening up . . . us Westerners can travel there so much more easily now . . . post-*perestroika* . . . changes are in the offing. I could be the writer who gets in and sees it up close."

He stopped. Alex was staring at him, his fork forgotten in the air halfway to his plate, as close to an expression of shock as his habitually composed demeanor ever came.

"David . . . what?"

"What do you mean, what--? I'm saying I'd like to come with you next time? I want to see the changes. I want to hear from you how things have changed in Romania since you were a kid."

"David," said Alex again. His voice sounded hoarse—perhaps with anger, perhaps with some other emotion, or perhaps he just needed to clear his throat. *But why would he be angry, anyway?* thought David with irritation. And what Alex said next didn't shed much light. "You have to find your *own* story. Romania—Romania is my story. Where do *you* want to go? What do *you* want to find out? You can't just . . . ride the coattails of someone else's story."

"I'm sorry, Dad—what? What the hell are you talking about?"

"I'm talking about how you're old enough now to find out what your own story is—what your own deep motivations are. Your own *desires*. What do you want— what do you really want in life?"

"What do you mean? You know what I want. I want to be a journalist—a writer. I want to tell stories."

"But how is that a desire?" said Alex. His fork now made it back to his plate, with a clatter. "That—*writing*— that is just a means to an end. What is the end? What is the thing you want to bring about through writing?"

"Since when is writing not good enough in itself?" David threw down his napkin; his appetite was gone. "I've never been good enough for you, have I, Dad?"

"David. Such histrionics. I asked a simple question."

"Yes. Simple. Maybe that's your problem, Dad. Maybe you oversimplify everything. God forbid anyone could *desire* anything that wasn't simple—anything that couldn't, say, be bought."

"Oh, that is not fair, David."

"Isn't it? Sorry. You didn't leave me much other place to go."

They had never been close correspondents, but after that evening they had stayed less in touch than ever, although David lived not twenty miles from Alex's condo in Beverly Hills. David told himself that he was tired of his father's insinuations. He had so often felt he was disappointing his father in some obscure way, and he was tired of that feeling. Screw his father and his father's sad-eyed reserve, his phony old-country affectations.

— DAVID —
WEDNESDAY, NOVEMBER 29, 1989

But now here he was, ready to depart after all on a flight from New York to Romania.

He stood at the airport at Delta ticket counter, waiting for the attendant to process his ticket. She had a perfectly made-up face and a perfectly bland demeanor. She was asking him questions in a low voice.

He was leaning over the counter, both hands clutching the edge. He was still drunk.

She was studying his visa. "Is Romania your final destination?"

"I hope not," he responded sarcastically.

"Yes or no, Mr. Martin?"

"Yes," said David.

"Are you traveling to Romania for business or pleasure?"

"Who knows? Maybe both," he replied.

"Okay. Well, try to stay out of trouble. You know you're flying to a Communist country." She handed him the flight papers and, in chilly, professional tones, wished him a safe trip and thanked him for flying with the airline.

On the plane, he took a window seat. He felt aggravated. He wanted a drink. Here came the attendant at last.

"What would you like to drink?" she inquired.

"What would *you* like to drink?" was his reply.

She flirted back. "I'd have a very dirty Martini."

David smiled broadly. "Then I'll have the same."

She left to get the drink. David opened his bag, took out a bottle of bourbon, and downed a healthy slug. He made a face.

"Dammit," he said, still grinning. By the time the attendant returned with his martini, he was asleep.

He woke to the sound of a flight attendant's voice announcing over the loudspeaker: *"Bun venit in Republica Socialista Romania.* Welcome to the Socialist Republic of Romania." His gaze swiveled to the window. It was early morning: a foggy morning. His first impression was that the airport landing-strip was deeply potholed. His second, as he watched through the window, was of tumbleweeds and a pack of half-wild dogs racing alongside the bumping plane. Through the thick fog, he could glimpse the airport a few hundred feet away. It featured a small terminal, no bigger than a Western superstore, built of reinforced concrete and with windows facing the runway. More than half had broken glass. It looked like a military compound. Two army airplanes were parked next to an adjacent building.

A bus sat on the tarmac waiting for the passengers. It was blue and white and looked brand-new, in contrast with everything else on the tarmac. A *Militia* (state police) car accompanied the bus.

The passengers rushed to board the bus. David took his time and found a seat. On the floor was a newspaper. He picked it up and stared at the front page. It was *Scanteia,* a national newspaper: the official voice of the Communist Party of Romania.

He was drawn by the details. He saw a large headline:

"*Vizita oficiala de prietenie a tovarasului Nicolae Ceausescu, presedintele Romaniei, cu liderul de la Moscova, Mihail Gorbaciov pe 4 Decembrie.* " David had only enough Romanian to recognize the names. Ceausescu was the Romanian dictator everyone had been talking about, and Gorbaciov was his Russian counterpart. He guessed a meeting was going to take place on December fourth.

At that moment, reality sank in.

"Holy shit, I'm finally here, in Romania." He folded the newspaper and put it away. He looked through the steamy window at rows of dead cornstalks in the surrounding fields.

He turned around to study his fellow passengers. He felt hung over and filmy. His eyes were bloodshot and his head ached mightily.

The faces were diverse: some young and beautiful; some old, wrinkled, and tired. He heard many different languages and the sound of someone laughing. A young mother next to him was talking to her child. She stood up and closed the window, saying a word that sounded like "current." He would learn that it was a Romanian expression for wind draft. For now, he listened without understanding a word. They looked at him and laughed. He looked back and mouthed a smile.

After a short trip they arrived at the terminal.

Everybody got off and headed toward the squat airport building to go through customs. There was a long line, and David hummed with impatience. The airport was unheated. He rubbed his hands to warm them up.

When his turn came, the customs agent was brusque. The agent put out his cigarette and opened David's bag, pouring out its contents with a careless motion. As he pulled out clothes, a camera fell toward the floor. David jumped to retrieve it.

"What the hell?" he said.

The customs agent picked the camera up off the floor and peered at it. "You must register professional camera with Customs," he said rudely. "Why do you have professional camera?"

"I like to take pictures," said David.

"Answer my question."

"*Auzi la asta, face poze!*" said the agent sarcastically and disrespectfully to another customs officer in Romanian. They all laughed.

David looked around. He saw soldiers with AK-47s and dogs. Everyone's luggage had received the same treatment. He figured he should play it safe.

"I sometimes sell articles I write," he mumbled.

"Please step aside," said the customs agent.

David followed him. The man still had his camera.

The customs agent stopped. "How much money do you have on you?" he asked.

"What does that have to do with it?" demanded David. But then he caught himself. "Not that much. I've got a few hundred in cash and the rest in traveler's checks."

"Traveler's checks? Ha ha…" what won't do you any good here.

"Fifty dollars will do for you, and next time bring a smaller camera," said the agent. "I should confiscate it, but I don't think you knew the rules."

"Okay," agreed David. He slipped the agent the money as inconspicuously as he could. He stuffed his clothes back in the bag, took the camera, and walked away. "Son of a bitch," he muttered.

Outside, the day was cool although warmer than David had expected for December in Romania. Old Romanian cars were parked in the airport lot in not-so-neat rows. They all looked the same. Identical make and model.

David hailed a taxi. He asked the driver if he was able to take him to Constanta. The driver spoke no English, so David asked a passing man to translate for him.

The driver agreed to take him to Constanta. Through the impromptu interpreter, he told David he was lucky there was no snow. The drive would take almost three hours.

As they drove to the seaside, David watched the countryside unrolling through the window. He felt as if he had traveled back in time. He saw villages, farms, children playing in the fields. As they got closer to Constanta, delicate hills appeared on the horizon and the road stretched far in front of him. He saw that the trees lining it were painted on the bottom with white paint.

Sped-up folk music was playing, to which the driver whistled along. David made a face. The driver gave a small smile and changed the station. David half-closed his eyes.

He had already felt richer than he was, he would later reflect. He already felt superior. He had had his teeth cleaned before the trip; he had bought new clothes. Was he trying to impress people he didn't even know? Was he trying to be more American than any other American; was he trying to look a part? What part?

The fact was, he had just wanted to check on his old man. He wondered why he could never figure him out. He and his father shared a connection without logic.

He knew that blood was never logical. But he wanted more than that.

His father had barely had a chance to meet Ana, David's wife, before she became his ex-wife. It was only after the falling-out with Alex that David had first met her.

She was a reporter at another suburban paper; they knew each other by sight from both covering the monthly meetings of the regional water board. David had first asked her out at the end of one particularly grueling evening. He found her cute, with her cat-eye glasses and her blond pigtail, but some degree of guilt and embarrassment had driven him to it as well. They had been seated next to each other at a meeting that had gone on so long and been so boring that he had actually fallen asleep. He had been listing into her personal space, head practically touching her lap, before he had woken up.

They had enjoyed each other's company and, after a year of dating, didn't see why they shouldn't get married. Ana was enthusiastic, energetic; David found her—at least at first—a good foil for him, a useful curb for his worst excesses of brooding or drinking. She got him outdoors, into the mountains, winter and summer. She biked, skied, hiked—was, in short, a true California golden girl. He was California-born and bred as well, of course, but she seemed more purely so. No residue of an earlier generation's "old country" clung to her.

They had been happy the first year, their marriage a

well-oiled, pleasantly humming machine. They had gotten a sheepdog, named him Brewster. But by the middle of the second year they had become to each other a book reread too many times, and by the end of that year their mutual keynote was faintly resentful boredom. They were still in sync enough to agree together that it was time to call it quits before the resentment flared from a mild tinge to something more vivid and definite.

The two of them had never exactly fought. Ana was too cheerful-natured to be able to sustain a fight for very long. Her style was more to withdraw, to take the measure of the tension in a room and then quietly absent herself—which irritated David to no end. Still, before they parted for good, she had been able to land a few observations. They had been appallingly similar to his father's. David was too apathetic, she complained. When he protested, pointing to his list of lifelong ambitions, she had shaken her head. She wasn't saying he didn't *care* about anything. It was more that he never seemed to fully take part in the present. He could never just *enjoy* anything—enjoy the moment—without it having to *mean* something huge.

Only when he was drunk, she said, did he seem to be able to enjoy anything without turning it over. And not always even then.

Especially not then, he thought wryly, remembering. As she'd know, he thought, if she'd ever really known him.

— DAVID —
THURSDAY, NOVEMBER 30, 1989

A village passed by the cab window. He saw children playing in front of the houses and in the fields. Old women, their heads covered with scarves, sold home-made gem in front of their houses, which were whitewashed, with tiled roofs. Large, gnarled trees lined the narrow two-lane highway.

Outside the village, the highway was flanked by tall trees; beyond the trees lay agricultural fields. The outlines of hulking machinery showed in the distance.

They arrived in Constanta early in the afternoon. The city was vibrant. Many people walked the streets. He noticed a long line in front of a market where people were standing to buy fresh produce.

The driver turned around to study David.

"Welcome to Constanta," he said in heavily accented English.

"Yes, yes indeed," replied David.

They drove deep into the city. Before he knew it, David saw that they had reached an old neighborhood. The streets were narrow, and the architecture had gone from Communist slabs to French neoclassical. This was an ancient part of town built on Roman ruins.

David was surprised, wondering how this neighborhood had survived the Communist demolition spree. It felt like an architectural oasis. He could glimpse the sea between two buildings: the Black Sea his father always talked about. A deep blue scratched by the waves.

It was a typical windy day in Constanta. The taxi rolled up in front of a white marble-façade hotel, an elegant old building facing the sea. Only a few stories high, it looked like a white wedding cake. The roots of century-old trees cracked the sidewalk in front of it. The balusters on the terrace were wrought-iron but rusted. Everything looked like a shabby version of La Belle Époque.

The driver stopped the car and turned to David. "This is Hotel Palace for you."

David checked-in quickly then let himself into his hotel room and closed the massive wooden door with his foot. One of his bags fell heavily off his shoulder. He dropped the others carelessly on the floor and took two steps toward the middle of the room. He dropped the room keys on the bed.

He sat on the bed. He was tired, unable to think. In

disbelief that he was finally there. His father's hometown.

The room had an inordinately tall ceiling and ornate moldings, but it was cold and in need of fresh paint, and the wall-to-wall carpet was threadbare. The window creaked open, and wind blew the curtains. David moved to towards the window. The day was sunny. He could see the faraway harbor and ships. It was the old port, he could hear the waves hitting the pier and the seagulls screaming. The air was crisp, and the smell of seaweed opened his sinuses. He took the bottle from his bag, poured himself a drink, carried it back to the window, took a sip, and put the glass on the windowsill. Captivated by the scenery he closed his eyes. The noise from the city and harbor sounded faintly. He basked in the fresh breeze coming into the room. David inhaled deeply, closed the window and moved back toward the bed.

He wondered what his father would make of his having come here. He hoped, perversely, that it would bother Alex. He indulged, for a moment, in a quiet burst of gleeful defiance.

———

EMMA

At the sound of a woman's footsteps, David, by the fireplace at Phillip's, turned to look down the hallway. He knew it was her before she appeared. Emma.

She didn't see him yet. He stared at her. She looked— just the same. Maybe a little more filled out, more womanly, less tired and pale. She wore a simple yet elegant black dress, cut to bare her right shoulder. Her expression was pleasant: different from the intensity of the old days. She would be in her late thirties now.

A white-gold necklace with a cross pendant hung around her lovely neck. She had always been beautiful—small of stature and twine-thin yet curvaceous: just the right proportions. Her hair was still wavy, chocolate-brown, lightly grazing her shoulders. Her porcelain face was delicate, with structured features.

She had the same gorgeous, playful smile. Her enticing, deep brown eyes gazed curiously at Phillip. David could still remember the taste of those strawberry-sweet, pouty, heart-shaped lips the last time he kissed her.

Phillip threw his arms around her, and she reached up to hug him back. He whispered something in her ear, and her face showed a flash of animation.

David watched, feeling stunned. The firelight stung his eyes. His world stopped revolving.

"Let me make the introductions!" cried Phillip. "This is David Martin. He's the new greatest guy around."

David stood up to look into Emma's eyes. Her smile froze on her face. Her crescent-shaped eyebrows went up.

"So this is the beautiful woman we hear so much about at the office," said David. It was hard to keep the sarcasm out of his tone. "You know you're famous?" He did a mock bow.

"David Martin," said Emma. Seeming unaware of his edge of irony, she stared at him with luminous eyes. She had the same sweet voice David had adored. "How very nice to meet you . . . again." She held his hand, shaking it a little too long as she gazed at him intensely.

David smelled cologne, fresh as if she'd just applied it. She still preferred masculine colognes.

"And this is Alex Martin," said Phillip, "David's father."

Alex grabbed Emma's hand and smiled at her, surprised and gentle. "Emma . . . Emma . . . Emma . . . . Even more beautiful than I remember."

"You know each other?" said Phillip. "This is amazing. I have to hear the story."

"Phillip, I wouldn't even know where to start," said Alex.

There she was, right in front of David's eyes, almost unchanged. The last time he had seen her, how unfathomably different everything had been.

All those times he had seen her picture on Phillip's desk at work. He had heard even before he got the job that she was married to Phillip. He had realized he must eventually meet her again, but he'd never had any idea what he would, or could, say.

He felt he stood on the edge of a precipice.

Emma and Phillip had retired to the sumptuous kitchen.

"Come here, you," said Phillip, grabbing her. "I missed you."

They shared a long kiss. "I missed you too," said Emma.

"How about I make you a stiff drink and you come join the party?"

"Let me go up to check on Nicholas," said Emma. "I'll be right back down."

"We're doing this truth-or-dare type thing where we expose our weaknesses for everyone to flog," said Phillip. "It's pretty fun. I think you'd really enjoy it."

Emma smiled vaguely at him and began to walk away.

"We call it the game of life played on the other side," said Phillip.

"I don't understand," said Emma over her shoulder. "You know I'm not into games and such."

"You'll figure it out. It's basically a no-rules and no-holds-barred confessional."

"All right," sighed Emma. "Why don't you bring me that drink?"

She moved into the hallway and began climbing the spiral staircase to the upper floor. Below it, Alex stood following her with his eyes.

The aroma of her perfume lingered in the room long after she had gone. Alex, too was mesmerized.

— ALEX —
FRIDAY, DECEMBER 1, 1989

Ten years earlier, Alex had been in a hospital room by the window, listening to the sounds of the sea: the slapping of the waves, the cries of the gulls. The room was clean and bare, with a large window which let in a profusion of honey-colored light.

Families were visiting patients outside in the courtyard. Alex watched them hugging each other. Dead leaves lay scattered in the alleys. Behind the wrought-iron fence, he could see the beach.

He heard steps in the hallway, getting closer. He recognized their cadence and turned with a smile.

Emma opened the door. She wore her hair long and had a clean, well-scrubbed face. She wore the white coat of her profession, medical doctor.

"Did anyone leave a message for me?" asked Alex.

"No," said Emma. "Are you expecting anyone?"

He looked outside at the animated people in the courtyard. "No, not really." He turned slightly, with a tiny smile. "Just, today seems like a nice day for a visit. That's all."

"That's why I came to see you before I went home," said Emma. She moved toward Alex with her hands on her hips. "So how are you today?"

"I'm good," said Alex. "Feeling better. You?"

"Besides tired, I'm okay. I just got off my shift." She came to stand beside him at the window.

"Busy day today?"

"Eh, no more so than usual," said Emma. She paused. "Well, perhaps a little sadder than usual. That man who lost his wife in the car accident they were both in: he's talking as if there's no point in going on. He says . . . he had a vivid way of putting it. He said he feels like just a piece of meat without her—now that he can't any longer look at the world through her eyes."

Alex shook his head. "It's tragic. How old a man is he?"

"Perhaps your age, in fact," said Emma. "He seems older than you, in looks. But by the chart, your age."

They were words in which it could have been possible to read a flirtatious intent, for all that Alex was old enough to be her father. But Emma was not flirting. The friendliness between her and Alex had always had a formal quality about it. They sensed in each other some rare mutual understanding, and each chose to handle that as if it were something fragile.

"I hope he will learn to live a full life without her," said Emma. "I know it won't come easily or happen soon, but I hope he does."

"Of course I hope so too," said Alex, "but I wonder how likely it is." He mused a moment. "In America, you know, the people are in love with the idea of change: we hear always how we can change for the better, how we can start anew, become different people, better people. I have always wondered if it was because I was European that I doubted this idea. I don't think people really change. Not fundamentally. If that man needs another's eyes to see through, he will always need them."

"Oh, Alex," said Emma. "I am European too, but I do hope you're wrong."

"I hope so too, my dear, in fact," said Alex, smiling down at her. "It's something I've been thinking of a lot lately. Thoughts of my family bring such questions to mind."

"Your family—yes. Your son, I should think?" Emma had heard Alex talk about David. He had never said a lot, but it had not escaped her attention that what he did say was always delivered in wistful tones. There was some deep regret there, into which she hesitated to pry.

"Yes—indeed, my son has been on my mind." He fell quiet a moment. "Well—you should go home and rest, after all." He turned back to the window. "I'll just stay here and enjoy the beautiful day."

"Okay then," said Emma, smiling. "I'll see you tomorrow."

———

The party was in full swing. Raucous laughter rose above a din of voices. The fire was roaring in the fireplace.

Emma was sitting on the floor by the fire, Phillip next to her. "I think I understand the game now," she said. "Would you like to see my ace?"

"If you're ready," said David, looking at her intently.

"My ace is fear and doubt," said Emma.

"Ah," said Phillip, a shadow crossing his face. "Well then. Tell us when you were most afraid."

"When it was too late to go back," she said. "Because I had dreamed dreams, and then when they turned out to be worthless, I couldn't go back to erase them." She moved closer to Phillip. Her face was very calm.

— EMMA —
FRIDAY, DECEMBER 1, 1989

Emma's apartment had been on the seventh floor of an apartment complex built in the early 1970s. It had been crumbling and nostalgic, her furniture a mix of standard-issue cheap new stuff and heirloom items. The walls, like the walls almost everywhere in the city, were in need of a fresh coat of paint, the floors covered by threadbare rugs. There were books, paintings, vinyl records, cassette tapes and flowers everywhere. The apartment had four bedrooms and two balconies, one facing the sea and the other the city.

Later, she wouldn't even remember how or when she had first made the decision to leave. She did remember not being sure for a long time if she had it in her. And she remembered how, now that she was so close, she had been afraid that her doubt would make her ruin everything.

She'd been in the shower when the Guide had come knocking on the door. She remembered how she had walked toward the door, drying her hair with a towel. "Come on in," she said as soon as she had looked through the peephole.

The Guide was a tall and muscular man dressed like a priest, his hair beginning to go gray. He and Emma took seats at the small kitchen table. He looked preoccupied. His eyes darted around the room.

"Did any of my neighbors see you when you got in the elevator?" Emma asked.

"No, I made sure I entered the building when no one was around."

"Great."

"Do you have a phone?" the Guide asked.

"Of course I do." She nodded toward the phone on the wall next to them.

The Guide immediately reached over to unplug the cord. He was afraid the Securitate would listen in. It was the secret police agency in Romania, part of the Department of State Security.

"Let's not waste words," he said. He was carrying a book that looked like a Bible. He opened the back cover and from a secret compartment pulled an envelope out and handed it to Emma. "Read through this carefully. When you're through, burn it."

Emma put the envelope aside.

"No, read it now," said the Guide. "I want to see you burn it."

Emma looked straight into his eyes, shook her head, opened the envelope, and began reading the pieces of paper inside it.

The man watched her for fifteen minutes as she read the letter. The only noise was the clock ticking on the wall and the kitchen faucet dripping slowly.

He lit a cigarette to calm his nerves. If they were caught, neither of them would have much of a future. They could end up in the state penitentiary for a very long time. Emma's career would be ruined.

Finally, she stood up and walked to the sink. She struck a match and burned the papers. When they were burned almost completely, she dropped them in the sink.

The Guide rose to his feet and threw them a glance.

"Did you understand the last paragraph?" he asked as he stood at her apartment door.

"Yes," said Emma. "It doesn't apply to me. I am not going to change my mind."

"Then I'll see you at the time and place," whispered the Guide.

"Yeah," said Emma. "Thanks."

The Guide opened the door slightly to see if anyone was on the hallway. After he assured himself he was alone, he put his hat on and left, closing the door behind him.

Emma fell deep in thought, biting the inside of her cheek.

Emma Grigo had lived her whole life in Constanta. It was the second largest city in Romania. An old port that survived the Greeks, the Romans and the Ottoman Empires. Situated right on the western coast of the Black Sea. Named Constanta after *Flavia Constantia*, the sister of the Roman Emperor *Constantine the Great*. Emma would reflect later that it had been a beautiful life in many ways, although a type of beauty best appreciated by a child, especially one who grew up protected and encouraged. She had been an only child of two gentle-natured parents who had also spent their whole lives in Constanta. They worked their whole careers in the secondary schools, her mother a biology teacher and her father a swimming coach.

As a child, Emma had loved spending time with her parents. She took after them, with her wry and quiet nature, and they often treated her less like a child than like a younger friend or devotee. She inherited her mother's interest in science. She had never been disgusted by worms or mice or dead animals; at four years old she would crouch and poke at them with a stick, fascinated by what she could see of their reactions and inner workings.

Her mother began encouraging Emma early on to become a scientist or better yet, a doctor.

"Why couldn't I be a teacher like you, mama?" Emma asked once at about nine years old.

"Teaching is good, but it's so much more special to be a doctor, my love. You could save people's lives! Doctors have the respect of everyone."

Emma couldn't imagine not going along with her parents' wishes. She had always considered their wishes the same as hers. It would be years before she would fully admit to herself how unhappy it had made her to pursue medicine as a course of study and a career. She excelled at it yet never quite enjoyed it. The academic pressure, the competitiveness, the swagger expected of medical doctors and students, never sat well with her.

Yet, she knew it was a good profession, and it made her parents happy. She found what satisfaction she could in, first, doing well in her coursework and, later, forming bonds with certain patients like the bond she had with Alex. She convinced herself she was happy enough, as a doctor.

But childhood was where she would go when she reminisced. To be a child in Constanta had not been a terrible thing. Children don't know what else the wide world holds. Just as she had been fascinated with her mother's work, so she had also adored accompanying her dad to the pool every day of summer vacation, when he was teaching summer classes at the school or the local kids center. She would spend all day in the pool. It was where she made her best friends as a child. The other kids liked her for her laughing good nature and the swimming tips and tricks she could show them. She could stay underwater longer than any of them, and she looked to them like some pale, graceful seal as she spun and rolled under the surface, coming up with barely a sputter.

She made friends also in the apartment building, spending long afternoons of make-believe in the courtyard, and at the beach, where she and her parents would go every weekend day in the summer. Also in the summer, they would go to visit one or the other set of grandparents out in the country. Here she could run, and swim, and daydream, and watch animals to her heart's content. In the country, as everywhere, other kids would gravitate to Emma because she seemed so good at amusing herself, and they, intrigued, wanted to join her. She never went looking for friends.

Outdoor girl though she was, she could be equally contented spending hours indoors by herself. Of course, there was the weekly three minutes of Saturday-afternoon cartoons on the government-run television station; she loved those as much as the next child and would desert the streets along with all the others as soon as one-o'clock struck. And then also, when the power would go out in the building or the block, she would sit by the window with a lit candle, watching people and cars on the boulevard. She would daydream, imagining that she was somehow controlling them. She would sometimes focus on one black-coated figure in particular, willing the person with all her might to stop at a certain store or turn at a certain corner. Sometimes it worked, and then she would experience a strange, heady, unsettling sense of power: thrilling precisely to the extent that she didn't know if she really wanted it—that godlike ability.

When she was about twelve years old, her parents arranged for her to begin taking piano lessons with Mihaela who lived upstairs, a brilliant concert pianist. Emma enjoyed the contemplative repetitions of learning the piano, and she couldn't help but notice as well that her parents seemed more at ease when they came home to find her practicing scales rather than sitting by herself in the dark.

So her child and teenage years had gone on, pleasant, dreamy, devoted. As high school went on, of course her girlfriends almost all found boys to go steady with, but Emma kept herself apart from those concerns. She listened with patient good cheer to their stories, but privately, she felt no interest whatsoever in pursuing love and romance. It seemed confusing to her, and somehow unbecoming. Her friends seemed to have to make themselves into different people when they encountered boys. It seemed to become all about how you could please another person. Emma—overlooking the extent to which she had already devoted herself to pleasing her parents—told herself half in jest that she supposed she was too selfish to date boys.

Soon after entering university, however, she met Robert. He was a good-looking boy, his blond hair and blue eyes presenting an intriguing contrast to her own looks. He was studying medicine as well, highly dedicated to the calling. Emma met him in biology lab, her first term.

She was drawn to his quiet ways, which seemed a match for hers. She would come to find out that in fact, his quietness was of a different kind. He seemed aloof on the surface but had a good heart beneath; he had, however, almost no sense of humor. When she would tell him of her flights of imagination as a child, he would blink in confusion; she soon stopped telling him anything she thought he might not understand and learned to tamp down her own tendency toward ironic observation.

She was fond of Robert, and she could see that from the outside, he and she appeared to be a wonderful match. And—inevitably—her parents adored him. So she told herself that the prickles of boredom she felt whenever she was with him were just signs of their familiarity with each other. It was comforting to have Robert in her life. And he was good for her in other ways as well. He was a better medical student than she was; he helped her with her work and inspired her to higher standards.

And then, in the fall of her third year at university, tragedy struck. Her parents, in the prime of their lives, were killed one afternoon when an out-of-control emergency vehicle rammed into the back of their car while they were running errands in the center of town.

Emma stayed in school. She would wonder later if it had been the right decision, but in any event, it was the one she took, and she could thank Robert for helping her to take it. He was the perfect companion in mourning, holding her all night sometimes without saying a word.

She had nothing to say either. She had grown so adept at keeping herself in check around him that she was mute now even in grief. She cried in his arms and took comfort from his body close to hers, but she couldn't talk to him about her memories of her parents. She couldn't talk to him about who they had been. And she couldn't tell him— she could barely even tell herself—how she was mourning not only the loss of them but the fact that they would now never see their dreams come true through her. She had dedicated her life to living their dreams, and now all of that was for naught. And she was left with no dreams of her own.

It was then—the year she was twenty years old and bereaved—that she had first begun to think about leaving the country and starting a new life somewhere else. The thought had first occurred during the numb weeks immediately following the accident. The government vehicle ramming the back of her parents' car and sending it spinning into the guardrail had reminded her of other stories she had heard, vaguely, over the years, of countrymen of hers whose lives had been forever disrupted by a knock on the door in the middle of the night. *Securitate*—the word that wove beneath every current of life in her country.

She had never paid it special mind before. It was a fact like the weather, and less interesting. But the idea that at any moment her life could be upended by an unexpected intrusion from a representative of the state had taken root in her mind for good. It would grow gradually over the years until it flowered in the bloom of a plan to escape.

In the meantime, she and Robert drifted apart. At the time, it did not seem to her that her leaving him had anything to do with the wish to rebel, the vague plans to escape. Certainly, though, of all the things she could never really tell him, this would be the prime example. She had even sometimes heard him speak in quite reverent tones of the state. He would talk about how lucky they were to have been born in a country that would pay for every part of their education, would support them as they pursued their true callings.

She and Robert parted ways. It happened quietly, subtly. By the end of her third year, he had begun to see someone else—a sweet but mousy girl a year behind them.

Emma continued with her medical studies. This was a practical decision in some ways; it would have been difficult for her to start all over again in another field of study, and she had done well enough in this one that it would be a shame to have wasted the work. She stayed with it in tribute to her parents, as well. On her desk at home, she kept an open locket with their pictures, alongside the Ioannes Korais icon that had been one of their most treasured possessions.

—— **EMMA** ——
FRIDAY, DECEMBER 1, 1989

After the Guide had left her, Emma needed to talk to someone. The secret was ballooning inside her. She went to visit Alex that night while on her shift, to tell him.

By night, Alex's room looked even starker. There was just one small lamp in the corner. The bed was untouched, still made with its severe corners. Alex leaned on the windowsill, legs and arms crossed.

Emma closed the door behind her and walked around the room, agitated. Alex thought she looked like she hadn't slept in a while.

"How well do you know the man?" asked Alex.

"Well enough to trust him."

"Enough to trust him with your life?"

"I have to. He's my only hope. Don't you see how things are here?"

"Emma, I see how things are here. But you want to cross the border with a man you've only seen twice in your life, a man whose real name you might even not know. How do you know he's not working for the Securitate? You know if you get caught, you're done. Your future is ruined. How do you know he's not going to take your money and turn you over to the Border Patrol? Or rape and kill you? How come he has all this information when nobody else here has any?"

"Look outside the window, Alex," said Emma. Her voice was a whisper. She was almost crying—angry, though not confused. "What do you see? The sea. And you know Turkey is on the other side. And you know what I see? Water. Because I am not allowed to *think* across the water. I am not allowed to think outside the borders. This is how things are here, and yes, you were right. People don't change much. But a person's place can change.

"And I want to change it. It is all I want. I've always dreamed of moving to America, ever since I was a child. I'm obsessed with this dream. Only if I can go to America can I meet Rhett Butler."

She said it with a smile on her face. *Gone with the Wind*

was her favorite movie. Then, suddenly, she started to cry.

Alex stared out the window, as if he could see what she saw across the sea.

Someone knocked at the door. Emma and Alex looked at each other, startled.

"*Intra.* Come in," called Alex. "Who can it be this late at night?" he said in a quieter tone.

David cracked the door and poked his head in. "Dad?"

"David?" cried Alex.

David entered, looking tired and disheveled. He gave Emma a brief look, taking in the white coat and doctor's nametag. The stethoscope lay on the bed.

David and Alex gave each other a hug. "You look good, Dad," said David. His gaze shifted to Emma. She smiled, embarrassed, and jammed her hands in her pockets.

"This is Emma. Emma Grigo," said Alex.

"Nice to meet you, Emma," said David.

Emma grabbed her stethoscope from the bed and moved toward the door. A look passed between her and Alex.

"I bet you two have a lot to talk about," she said. "I was heading out anyway."

"You can stay," said David.

"I'd love to, but I must finish my rounds."

"Finally, someone who can speak English to me."

"Yes, I've studied it since fifth grade," said Emma with a smile.

It was enough to see her smile once for David to remember it forever.

"Well, I hope to see you again, Doctor," said David.

"Of course," replied Emma. She closed the door behind her.

She would remember how at that moment, something was slowly breaking inside of her. She had left heavy, burdened. She was the loneliest woman in the world.

———

At the party, Emma gazed at David, lost in thought.

"Do you still fear?" asked Alex.

"I do, but not like that," replied Emma. "Fear is like pain; it goes inside you and changes with you. In time you get used to it, and you don't feel it anymore, although you know it's there."

"Well, look what she did with her fear," said Phillip. "She crossed an ocean and more. She made a loving family and started a fabulous business. I think she wins already. I think she gets to keep her ace."

"Then she'll call the shots now," said David.

"I don't want to be the one calling the shots," said Emma.

"You must obey the rules, dear," said Phillip.

"You might be wrong, Phillip," said David. "If she calls the shots, it means she doesn't have to obey the rules— including that one."

"Well, we're playing jagged, remember?" said Phillip. "I say we watch what happens if she plays until she loses her ace."

"Okay, Phillip," sighed Emma. "So what do I have to do?"

"Ask anyone you want to show you their ace."

"Then I want to see David's ace," she said, staring at David with those big brown eyes.

"That's easy," said David. "My ace is curiosity."

"Curiosity, yes," said Emma, musing. "And how far has your curiosity taken you?"

"It's taken me everywhere. So far, sheer luck has brought me back in one piece and unharmed. Well . . . generally speaking."

THE ENCOUNTER

— DAVID —
FRIDAY, DECEMBER 1, 1989

The Palace hotel had been old, built in the Romanesque style, with an ornate façade. There were big old oak trees in front. The marble stairs, just like everywhere here, were cracked.

David stood in front of the hotel, studying a map. Finally, feeling disoriented, he decided to walk.

The night was chilly. It was still early in the evening, and the streets were packed with people walking in all directions. He walked down a large boulevard lined with birches. Across the street were brand-new apartment buildings, some still under construction. The style was boxy and utilitarian, the construction site dirty and cluttered. To the left were a row of older buildings, more elegant, some decaying and some well-maintained. The street was partially lit only by streetlamps; darkness lay over the buildings.

The buses and bus stops were packed with people. Children played happily in the front courtyards of apartment buildings. The adults, for their part, were grim, stern. The Communist regime had taken a visible toll on them.

He noticed that the people were dressed all but identically. No one individual stood out. The women wore long coats and fur hats made of rabbit, sheep, or, for the relatively more privileged, arctic fox. The men wore coats of sheep leather with wool or astrakhan hats. Clothes didn't betray social class here, just as he'd heard. Everyone dressed and behaved the same.

David stopped under a light in front of an open gate. He checked the address one more time. He passed through the gate and entered the same hospital park Alex had seen from his room. He stopped and looked around, then started up the spiral staircase. At the top, he tried a door and found it open.

The hallway was dimly lit. David pulled his notes from his pocket to check on the room number. There were doors on both sides of the hall, all closed. He found Room 304 and saw light creeping from beneath the door. He heard voices, bits of conversation. He didn't know what to do. He leaned close to the door, then knocked.

"*Intra*," came Alex's voice.

David poked his head in to see Alex by the windowsill. Alex uncrossed his hands and arms and made a sudden move, as if startled.

"Dad?" said David.

"David?" said Alex.

David saw Emma and sensed he had interrupted something delicate. He would remember how uncomfortable he had felt and how he had wanted to leave but how she was a step ahead of him. She had left before he could say anything.

His dad, though, was mellow.

"This is a good one on me, David," Alex had said after Emma had gone. "It's safe to say I didn't expect you to show up here. How long have you been in country? Was it hard to find this place?"

"I flew in this morning," David told him. "My hotel isn't that far. I just came by to check the place out. The doors weren't locked, so I showed myself in. You'll get an official visit tomorrow, flowers and everything. I hope I didn't interrupt anything, though."

"Oh, Emma's great," said Alex. "She's the doctor on duty at night, and I'm an insomniac. We got to know each other."

He stared at David. It had been so long since they had last seen each other. "I'm really glad to see you here, David."

"Me too, Dad. But this is crazy. I'm here to take you home."

"I'm already home. I'm well taken care of here."

"Here we go again," said David. "Nonsense. You've lived in California forty-five years, you didn't come back here for the first forty of them, and suddenly this feels like home?"

"I was born here," said Alex. "That's enough for me to call it home. The time felt right, so I came back, and now I want to stay a while. The Communism doesn't bother me. What's wrong with that?"

"What's wrong? You got sick, and I had to travel for twenty-four hours to get here to make sure you're all right."

"I didn't ask you to come here, David, but I'm actually glad you did." Alex sat down on the bed.

"Do you know why I came?" he went on. "This place is part of me. This is where everything began for me."

David stayed standing. "What began here? You left so long ago."

Alex stood and went to the window. He stayed there,

admiring the reflection of the full moon on the water.

"My ambitions would have always grown bigger than this place," said Alex, not really answering the question. He paused as if uncertain what to say next. "For years," he went on, "I feared coming back to see what I'd left behind. But then it all faded out, except for the curiosity.

"And I don't know how to explain it, David. It's something strange, the energy here. Everything is magical for me, yet everything seems normal. I'm connected with the land and everything surrounding me. This chaos is me! That's who I am. That's why I say I belong here. I'm not delusional, son."

David was taken aback at Alex's burst of sincerity.

"Maybe one day I'll understand," he said. "I always you knew you were fascinated with this place, but now I see how much. Just remember, California is still your home too.

"You know," he went on, jocularly, "I'm curious as well. About the little doctor."

"What about the doctor?" said Alex. "She's a very smart woman."

"And good-looking too," said David.

"I take it you're gonna come see me often now," said Alex with a smile.

"You got it," said David. "The official visit, with

flowers, tomorrow morning. What time does she get off her shift?"

"You're incurable," said Alex.

SATURDAY, DECEMBER 2, 1989

It was a chilly Saturday morning. The streets were almost empty. David walked down the same road near the harbor that his father had run along as a little boy decades before. He climbed the same hill. The view was breathtaking.

He stopped at a small bakery. From the limited options he chose a pretzel with poppy seeds and a cup of *Sana* buttermilk. It looked like everyone else in the bakery had ordered the same thing.

While he ate his pretzel, he stared at a few kids dressed in school uniforms playing tag in front of the bakery. They must be late for school, even though it was Saturday. He had read that the education system in Romania was rigid and strict, emphasizing discipline above all. The curriculum was heavily influenced by Communist doctrine.

He walked past the same house where Alex had lived before departing for America--where he had seen the car. The house and the garden were still there, but they were renovated, gleaming in the morning light. The property now belonged to a party higher-up.

He wasn't sure what he should feel, looking at all of it. None of it suggested itself as a clue to his father's heart.

In front of the hospital David stopped by a flower stand and bought a beautiful bouquet of purple and white orchids. He rushed into the hospital.

As he was standing in the hallway with the flowers behind his back, Emma came into view. He went up to her and pushed the bouquet right into her nose.

"For me?" said Emma, looking shocked. She took the bouquet slowly. "How nice. What is the occasion?"

"No occasion," said David. "I'm just trying to bribe you."

Emma smiled, charmed. "I accept. What do I have to do in return?"

"Have dinner with me. I'd like to get to know you."

"You know I'd love to, but I can't." She smiled sheepishly. "Do I have to give the flowers back now?" She buried her nose in the orchids.

"No," said David. "They really bring out the color of your eyes."

They walked down the hallway. David gazed at her as she gazed straight ahead.

"Aren't you supposed to be visiting your father?" she said.

"I will," said David. "But right now I'm visiting you."

"I was just leaving," said Emma. "My shift is over. I'm really tired."

"It's a beautiful day," said David. "I'll walk you to your car."

Emma pushed open the exit door, smiling. "I don't have a car."

"Then I'll walk you home."

Clouds and sun chased each other, and the clouds seemed to be winning. But to David, it was a glorious morning. He and Emma walked, not fast, giddy with talk.

Emma's English was excellent. And she wasn't like any woman David had known before. Independent and strong-minded, sure—but also so romantic and so given to storytelling. He wasn't used to that combination. And she made it clear she wanted to please him, to make him laugh.

As they walked through the streets, she showed him all her childhood haunts: the candy store that still stood, although cobwebs could be discerned at the corners of the display window; her old primary-school playground; the fence she and another mischievous friend had hurdled to sneak into an apartment building to play pranks.

"What sort of pranks?" teased David.

"Oh," said Emma, "we had a name for it, but I don't

know if you have it in English. You run up to the door—knock knock—and run away . . . ."

"Ding dong ditch!" said David.

Emma laughed at the name, repeating it. "*Ding dong . . .* so you play that in America as well!"

"Of course we play that in America," laughed David. "Kids must play that all over the world."

Emma kept laughing. They walked down a street surrounded by chestnuts trees on each side. Then she slowed as they neared her building.

"This is C1. My apartment building," she said.

"Ah, this is it," said David. He took a step back and looked up. It was a tall building—eight or ten stories. "You know," he said, "I can settle for coffee instead of dinner."

Emma looked at the bouquet in her hands and laughed. "I forgot you bribed me. Come on. I'll make you some coffee."

They walked through the trees at the front of the building and down a narrow alley that split the front courtyard in two. They greeted two old ladies seated on benches in front of the building. As they walked by, the old ladies started gossiping in Romanian. David had the feeling they were talking about him and Emma.

They went up a short flight of stairs and into the

building. Emma went to the elevator and pushed the button. Nothing happened.

"Shit, this elevator never works. Ready for some exercise? I'm on the seventh floor."

"Let's do it," replied David. "It'll be good for me. Too much drinking lately."

On the stairs in her building, she turned to David, a finger to her lips. "Don't talk," she whispered.

David said nothing, but his curiosity was piqued.

"This is me, number thirty-two," said Emma theatrically.

Once they were inside, she locked the door immediately. "Make yourself comfortable. I'll go change, then make the coffee." She disappeared into the bedroom.

David walked around the apartment, snooping. Everything seemed very clean—and also as if there were a story behind it. He noticed all the unique furniture and oil paintings. There was a formal living room with black shiny furniture and green cushions. It looked mid-century modern. There was a big dining table in the middle covered by a hand-crafted macramé crochet. It looked old but neatly preserved.

An old silver frame painting hung in the center of one wall. David's curiosity drew him closer. It was signed "Grigorescu."

"Wow you own a Grigorescu!" called David. "I know those are hard to come by."

"It's been in my family for over sixty years," Emma responded from the other room.

In the living room, he saw a glass cabinet filled with icons. He bent to look more closely at one of them. The icon, which looked very old, depicted Saint George killing the dragon.

A mirror lined the back of the cabinet. Looking in it, he saw the reflection of a small piece of luggage behind the couch: a knapsack. He turned and went to the couch to investigate further. On top of the knapsack was a bundle of official-looking papers and dollar bills wrapped in watertight plastic.

He walked to the window. "You've got a nice view," he called.

"Just a second," replied Emma. "I'll be right out."

"No rush," said David.

He spotted a wood-frame TV and turned it on. There were only six channels displayed on the front panel. He switched between the channels but soon realized there was only one TV station. A news anchor was talking. David could catch the odd word and name and surmised that the man was talking about the Fourteenth Communist Party and the fourteenth consecutive unanimous re-election of the party leader, Nicolae Ceausescu. Despite Ceausescu's growing international isolation, Romania's state-controlled television continued to lionize the "genius of the Carpathians. "

"Oh, please turn that off," called Emma. She came into the hallway, brushing her hair. "I'm so sick and tired of hearing about him. You know, this entire society is under the grip of its own frustrations and unable to find a successor. He's been ruling Romania since 1965."

"It seems like things are getting very unstable in the Eastern bloc," said David. "The Berlin Wall fell less than a month ago. Romania could be next, hey?"

"Everyone is afraid of tomorrow," said Emma, still following her own train of thought. "It's not the Golden Age anymore. We might be in Europe, but we're so secluded. This regime is killing us. Do you know that he was just reelected last month for yet another five-year term? I don't think Romania is next. I don't believe there are serious internal threats to Ceausescu's continued totalitarian rule."

"Was he the only one on the ballot?"

"Yes, can you believe that? That's probably unimaginable for you. You know, I can't even speak to you about this. I could spend years in jail for talking to you about this."

"Then I guess enough politics," said David. Emma retreated back into her room.

He wandered into the kitchen. Things in there seemed less clean. He saw two cups of coffee on the kitchen table and an ashtray with two different brands of cigarette butts. Turning, he saw a film of spilled coffee on the stove.

He looked in the sink and saw the burnt papers. He peered at them closely.

The bits of conversation he'd overheard when he was standing outside Alex's hospital-room door came back to him. *Trust him with your life . . . ?* And Emma: *My only hope . . . . . Alex saying, whose real name you might not even know . . . Border Patrol . . . information . . . .*

His train of thought was interrupted by Emma's voice. "Ready for coffee?"

"Yep," said David.

She busied herself at the stove. David sat in a kitchen chair and studied her.

"I see you enjoy art," he said. "You have a lot of collectible pieces."

"Yes, I've always enjoyed art," said Emma. "I like all art but am most attracted to paintings and old icons."

"I saw your Saint George icon. It's remarkable. A thing like that, you don't see every day."

"It's an Ioannes Korais," said Emma. "It's over two

hundred years old. My family has had it for years."

"It must be worth a lot of money," said David. "Would you consider selling it?"

"I never thought about it," said Emma, "and anyway I wouldn't want to get in trouble with the authorities."

"You might need the money someday."

Emma turned at the stove to face him. "What makes you think I'd need the money?"

"Just a wild guess."

"Seriously, I don't need the money."

"You might need it more than you think."

"What is it you're trying to say?"

"Take another wild guess, Emma."

"It's not for sale, David. But you know something? I'll give it to you. For free."

She turned the burner off under the coffeepot, and he followed her into the living room. She went to the curio cabinet, opened the glass door, and bent to take the icon out. She froze a moment, and he could see that in the mirror she had glimpsed the bag with the package wrapped in plastic on top of it. The package had fallen on its side.

She turned to David, clutching the icon in her hand.

David took the icon. He touched it lovingly. He didn't know what to say. It was a precious item, and he barely knew Emma.

"Why are you giving this to me? It's got a lot of meaning for you."

"It did," said Emma.

"I can't accept this! You may have gotten to know my father well, but you and I are almost strangers."

She turned to the window. She put her fingers to her mouth to try to stop the tears, but she couldn't stop them. She turned to David.

He touched her face. "I don't know just what you're doing," he said, "but I know it's hard to let go of things that you knew all your life. Especially if they've been part of your family."

"If I give it to you," said Emma, "at least I know one piece of me will get to America. It will have a longer life there. My future is so uncertain. I can see that you admire it. You see beauty in little things. I'm certain you'll take care of it."

"Of course I will, but . . . it just doesn't seem right."

"I'm tired," said Emma. She looked up at David. She seemed suddenly so fragile. David hugged her, awkwardly. He didn't want to make the wrong gesture, give her the wrong idea.

She disengaged and wiped her eyes.

"You don't have to explain now," he said. "We'll talk again soon."

Emma gave him a long look.

"I think I should go now," he said. "I'll see you again—very soon."

"Please be careful," said Emma. "Don't talk to anyone; don't let people notice you're a foreigner. I am serious. This is not Los Angeles."

"I will. I promise!"

He left, closing the door behind him.

Emma turned to look outside the window. It had started to drizzle. The sky was gray and dark. She could see the leafless treetops shaken by the wind. Farther on, she could see the deeper, angry gray of the sea. It was a twirl of foamy water dashing against breakwaters and piers. She felt desolate.

Out on the street, it was rainy and cold. David's hair was wet. He walked fast yet felt precisely attuned to what was going on around him. There were large potholes he must avoid. There were massive trees and beautiful, unkempt old buildings. The city seemed to be stuck in time, yet expectant. He heard chatter at every corner in which he could make out the words "Ceaucescu" and "Moscow."

He found himself in front of the hospital gate. He walked in. There was no one outside; the place was deeply quiet. He walked down the now-familiar hallway, stopped in front of the door, thought for a second, and then knocked.

"*Da, intra!*" called Alex.

In the room, Alex was reading in a chair by the window. He took his glasses off as David came in.

"You're wet," were his first words. "There are towels in the bathroom. Right across the hallway. Go dry yourself."

David removed his coat, shaking it to get rid of the excess water. Then he went into the bathroom to dry his hair.

He saw that the appliances in the bathroom were old, but the space was clean. The window was broken, letting in frigid outside air. White square tiles covered the wall from floor to ceiling. The light fixture was missing, the bulb uncovered. The toilet had a suspended reservoir with a chain; the paint on the reservoir was beginning to crack. There were rust stains on the fixtures.

He returned to the room, towel still in hand. "You're not too shabby here," he said.

"If that had mattered, I wouldn't be here," said Alex.

"Do you always have to be so uptight?"

"So, what do you think?" said Alex, ignoring the question. "How do you like it here so far?"

"It's different. I don't know what kind of

different. Yet."

"It's the kind that *you* are. You like different."

"I can't say yet." Unbidden, David took a seat on the bed. "So what's going on with that doctor of yours?"

"What do you mean?"

"Come on, Dad, you can tell me. You know I have a keen sense of smell when it comes to trouble."

"What do you want to know? She's a complicated and sensitive woman."

"I had coffee with her this morning."

"Since you already know her, why don't you ask her?"

"I'm asking you." David paused. "I think she wants to leave the country, and I think you've got something to do with it, and I think you're putting ideas in her head."

"That's ridiculous."

"How is it ridiculous? What it is, is dangerous, Dad. You could get her imprisoned or even killed. You must see how tense things are in this part of the world right now. Look at what's happening in Poland and now Ceausescu's visit with Gorbachev. We're sitting on a ticking regime bomb. I don't think you should encourage her."

"What makes you think I am, David?"

"Isn't it the truth?"

"No, it's not," said Alex. "I talked to her about it, but she had already made up her mind. And anyway, how do you know what she's planning?"

"I just figured it out," said David. "I plan to go see her again tonight. I know she's not working."

"You might want to stay away from her, David. You're a foreigner. You could mess up whatever plans she has."

"Remember, I like different. Maybe this is part of my story that you said I had to find. Maybe I want to find my connection with your birthplace. But I promise you I'll be careful."

Alex stared at him pointedly and then shifted in his seat. "So—what's going on back home? How is everybody?"

"Everyone sends you their love," said David. "No one's gotten married, more like everyone's getting a divorce. Mom's happy, though. Husband number three seems to be working out fine for now."

Alex laughed. Talk of home was safer ground. "We'll see how long that lasts. But maybe it will. Maybe she finally found someone crazier than she is."

David would remember that they had talked for a long time. David had never known that his father, at fifty-three, could still seem so young. He felt glad he had come, glad he could see the relaxed, funny side of his father.

Amazingly, Alex gave him Emma's phone number, and

David called her that night. He convinced her—with not that much difficulty, truth be told—to see him.

There was something inside of her that he liked a lot, although he couldn't put it into words. The feeling was new and vibrant, powerful. He had known Emma just a day, and yet the connection between them was intense. A clear attraction. He desired her—and desired to know more about her. She was a fruit he wanted to taste.

THE CASINO

Dressed in a nice black suit with no tie, David managed to take a cab to Emma's apartment. On the seventh floor he stared at her door, frozen before he could knock. Should he ring the doorbell, or should he have called first? Perhaps it was horribly impolite not to have called her before leaving to come over here.

He began to giggle, softly. He was feeling hysterical, packed with mixed emotions. He pressed the doorbell once. His hands twitched. No one came to the door. The hysterical feeling grew.

A few seconds later, he heard her voice. "Coming…"

David exhaled. Emma opened the door.

"Well, hello, David," said Emma, smiling. "You almost pass for a gentleman. That suit looks good on you.

"Shall we?" she went on. "It's a short walk."

"What made you change your mind about having dinner with me?" teased David as he and Emma walked down the street.

"How do you know I changed my mind?" Emma teased back. "Perhaps I am only directing you to the restaurant. What, you can't dine alone?"

David shook his head, laughing. "You wouldn't do that."

"Do what?" pressed Emma, mock-innocent. "You wouldn't be alone long. Haven't you noticed all the beautiful women here, only too happy to make a handsome foreigner's acquaintance?"

They stopped for a second, still giggling.

"Are we there yet?" said David with a smile on his face. They had reached a busy square, Ovidiu Square.

"You see, this is the statue of Ovid," said Emma. "You know, the Roman writer who died in exile here. You should probably take a photo with this statue. Something for you to write about. After all, aren't you here for some photojournalism?"

"Maybe so and maybe not," replied David with a smile. "Seems like I get the company not only of the most amazing doctor but a great tour guide as well."

"Such a bargain!" cried Emma.

David stopped to load his camera and take a snapshot of the statue.

"What is the building in the back?" he asks.

"That's the Museum of National History. Whatever is left of it. The regime makes its own history." She said the last in a whisper.

He took a picture of that building as well.

She was growing on David. The sky was full of stars, yet all he could look at was her. She saw so much beauty in little things. She was so unique.

They reached a waterfront promenade. A full moon was reflected in the agitated sea. The wind intensified as they neared the shoreline.

"This is the old Tomis," said Emma. "It's the oldest part of town and probably the oldest inhabited city in Romania. What you see in the distance is Tomis Port. We're almost to the restaurant. Right there."

She pointed to the end of the promenade, which was lit up by lamps. The white rail was getting soaked as the waves broke along the coastline.

"A long time ago," she said, "that was a real casino. Now the top floors are closed almost all the time. The restaurant is the main attraction. I'm telling you, it's a good one. It's been here since 1903. Once, it was our country's own Monte Carlo."

"It could be the French Riviera," said David. "Do I need a tie?"

"No, you just need me," she said.

"Two days in the city, and already I've met just the right person."

He offered her his arm. She smiled and took it.

The building was majestic, with columns and Art Deco arches above the door. The windows were large, brightly lit, and shaped like shells, and lion's-head gargoyles gaped from the roof. It perched on a cliff overlooking the Black Sea, with panoramic views of the ancient harbor of Constanta. You could hear the waves breaking on the wharf.

Inside, the décor was sumptuous: large spiral staircases which displayed a level of opulence unheard of in any other casino in Romania, marble floors, sparkling Art Nouveau chandeliers, stunning ceiling accents, and moldings and balusters of finely sculpted wood.

"Wow," said David, gaping. "Who would have thought . . . ? You're good at surprising people."

Emma smiled. "After all, I was bribed." She paused. "Do me a favor. When we get in, please don't speak until we get seated. I don't want the Securitate to find out I'm bringing foreigners here. I'm trying to avoid drama."

"Yes, boss," replied David.

They checked their coats, and a maître d' escorted them to a table. The restaurant was a true throwback to the pre-Communist era. The tables were set with white linen; the lights were dim. The music of Brahms played, and the walls were painted with zodiac signs. The atmosphere was intimate, romantic.

Emma and David were seated at a table by the window, overlooking the sea.

"This is all so beautiful," said David.

"I like this place," said Emma. "It reminds me of the old times." She paused. "Time here doesn't matter. It stands still. My grandmother used to tell me stories about this place."

"Share one, please."

"There are lots of legends about this place. One that I remember my grandmother used to tell me was about how the casino was built. They say it was built by a navigator whose daughter died at only seventeen years old. Her father, the story says, decided to build the Casino for young people to share the moments that his daughter couldn't. If you look from the top down, the casino it's supposed to look like a hearse and the windows like graves."

"That's fascinating," said David. "So are you close to your family?"

"I used to be. Not anymore." She turned to look out the window. "My parents died a while ago, in my third year at the university. I have some family left, but they don't live here."

"I'm sorry to hear that," said David.

"I'm used to it," said Emma. "What about you?"

"Well, you know . . ." said David. "My mom is in San Francisco with husband number three. I've got a dog and an ex-wife."

"You're lucky," said Emma. "I don't even have a fish."

"You must have a lot of friends."

"I know a lot of people. I've lived here all my life."

"Why do you want to leave, Emma?" said David abruptly.

Emma gave him a long, hard look. "What do you mean?"

"Emma," said David, "you know that I know—"

"What do you know?" she broke in. "You know nothing."

"Emma, you have roots here. And anyway, it's too dangerous."

"My roots are dead. There is nothing that can make me want to live here." She paused. "You forgot your icon this morning. It's still at my apartment."

"I wasn't thinking about the icon when I left," said David. "You made me forget about the coffee too."

"Well, I'm not going to let you forget to order."

She handed him the menu. He opened it and frowned.

"I can't read it," he said.

"Then I'll call the shots," said Emma. "I'll order for you too."

They relaxed as the food arrived and they drank more wine. The music turned to romantic jazz. After finishing their meal, they lit cigarettes.

"You know, these can kill us," said Emma looking at her cigarette.

"It's OK we'll die together!" responded David lighting it up.

Emma left hers to ash a moment and took another sip from her glass. "What do you think of this wine?" she asked. "Some visitors find it too sweet."

David took a small sip, as if to consider her question carefully. "On the contrary," he said. "I'd call it quite tart. Although to be honest, I'm not a wine person."

"It's both somehow, isn't it?" said Emma with a mysterious smile. "That is what makes our fine Romanian wine so special. It manages to be both sweet and tart at once."

"It's not the only thing at this table that's like that," said David, laying his hand over hers. She did not withdraw it.

"Ah, you're funny," smiled Emma. "But you know, in some vintages it's as if the sweet and the tart cancel each other out, and all that is left is bitter. Yet we still drink those bottles. We pay tribute to the insight that comes to you from being drunk on those bitter vintages. We call it 'bitter light.'"

"Bitter light," repeated David. "That doesn't make much sense. Yet it's a beautiful phrase."

"Well, that's our people for you—and our wine," said Emma, raising her glass. "Nonsensical but beautiful."

They toasted.

Emma looked at David with a seductive twinkle in her eye. "So what's next?" she said.

"Dance with me," said David.

"David!" she said, amused.

He stood and took her hand, raising her up. He held her at the waist and gazed at her, his face close to hers.

She stopped smiling. They stared at each other intensely.

"There's no dancing here," she said.

They shrugged and let the moment pass. But the spark

did not disappear. For two more hours they sat and talked.

"The band has left," said Emma. "I've lost count of how many glasses I've had. What a good time I'm having!"

David turned and saw the restaurant almost empty. Staff people were vacuuming tables and floors.

"This is how I always want to live," said David, "just keep going till everyone has left, till the band is gone and the cleaners are finished, just me and an old friend like you."

"Wouldn't that be nice," said Emma, "but maybe not here. Maybe somewhere on the other side of the ocean."

"To making it count!" said David, raising his glass.

Emma raised hers as well but quickly lowered it. "It's getting late," she said. "Let's go home."

At the coat check, David stood behind Emma and helped her into her coat. Just before he let go of her shoulders, he bent down and breathed a puff into her neck. She stretched back; he kissed her. She wrapped her coat around her.

Back at her apartment, he closed the door with his foot. He pulled her toward him and began to kiss her passionately, urgently. Her overcoat fell to the floor.

They kissed with still more passion. Emma kicked off her shoes. Her fingers traced a tattoo on David's chest.

Their hands intertwined.

When they made love, they were tender, feline, lithe. They were two equals and they knew it. After, they spent time in one of the covered balconies overlooking the city. They stared at the starts talking about their lives, smoking and giggling until morning hours. A sky full of starts and yet he was staring at her realizing how much he wanted to be with her.

———

At Phillip's house, the party crowd had thinned. Emma, David, Alex, and Phillip were still sitting around the fire. Each was trying to appear relaxed, but each had much to think about.

Phillip stood up. "Who would like a drink?"

"More wine for me, please," said Emma.

Alex threw a look at Emma and David. "I need a refill too," he said. "I'll come with you."

David and Emma were left alone.

"I wasn't really prepared to meet you," said David. "Maybe I should have been, but I wasn't."

"Our timing has always been bad," said Emma, "and this time is no different." She paused. "You didn't change much."

"I've often wondered about you," said David. He looked around. "You've done well for yourself."

Emma looked at David, hard and tenderly. She looked as if she would touch him with her eyes.

"I always knew I would marry someone like Phillip," she said.

"Then tell me something, Emma," said David. "Is this what you had in mind? Was it all worth it for you?"

Emma frowned as if put off by the question. "I don't know. I think it is. I've no regrets."

David looked at her intently. "You know, Emma . . . I want you to know that I wish I had done things differently then. I don't know what to call what we had, but it was great. I can't extinguish the memory."

"What we had was, we were lovers," said Emma. "With Phillip I have something different. It's called a relationship."

David was taken aback. She had said it gently, but it still rang like a rebuff.

Wistfully, he said, "What we had was definitely something else. I was not the perfect one for you, but I tried, in my imperfect way. I could fall in love with you again with my eyes closed."

"You need to let it go," said Emma. "Things are different now."

MONDAY, DECEMBER 4, 1989

It had been a sunny day by the seaside, crisp and bright. David and Emma were walking down the beach near the hospital, while Alex sat nearby on a stone bench. Emma wore jeans, a black wool pullover, and gloves with tips cut off; David had on a dark jacket, a black wool hat, and his backpack s slung over his shoulder.

They were alive with youth and happiness. David stopped and took Emma in his arms and lifted her off the ground. She threw her head back with laughter and hugged him, hard.

"You should see this place in the summer. It's so vibrant."

"I bet," David responded.

"Hi, Alex!" called Emma, playfully. "Isn't this day gorgeous? I love this weather. It's my favorite kind."

Alex patted the bench. "Come sit down."

In moving to sit, David dropped his bag. His camera tumbled out into the sand.

"Shit!" he said. "I can't break that." He picked up the camera, wiping the sand off. "Hey," he said. He pointed the camera at Emma. She assumed a cute position, chin resting on her hands.

"Oops," said David. "No film." He deftly loaded it and then pointed it at the sea and shot.

Emma sat down next to Alex, and they watched David as he busied himself with his camera.

"You're even more beautiful when you're happy," Alex told her.

"Oh, Alex," she said, smiling and shaking her head.

Alex stood. "Sit there, David." He pointed to the bench. "I'll take a picture of you."

David sat. Alex fiddled with the camera as David grabbed Emma's shoulders. Her head fell against his chest as she laughed.

"Perfect," said Alex. The camera clicked.

Later that afternoon in Emma's apartment, she sat cross-legged on the living room sofa, the photograph that Alex had taken in her hand. "I don't want to lose this picture."

David sat in an armchair, jotting notes on a legal pad. The icon was on the coffee table in front of them.

David's pen stopped. "Tape it on the back of the icon," he said. "That way I for sure won't lose it."

"I guess I can do that," said Emma. She bent over the table and affixed the photograph to the back of the icon. "What are you writing there? You've been writing for a while."

"Oh, it's just notes for an article."

"What kind of article?"

"I don't know yet. I have a lot of ideas. I'm not clear yet what I want to write about."

The phone rang. It was right next to David. He threw Emma a questioning look. She didn't move. Few more rings.

"Aren't you going to get that?" said David.

Emma stood, brushing past him as she picked up the phone. "*Da?*"

David could hear a man's voice on the other end although not the exact words. Emma's face dropped, and she began to fidget.

"*Da, bine, am inteles,*" she said. "Okay. Okay then. See you in church in two days."

She hung up the phone. The color had drained from her face.

David put his pen down. "You all right?"

"I have to go to church in two days."

David looked confused.

"That was the code message. It means I'll be leaving in two days."

David was silent. He put down his pad and pen. Never

taking his eyes from Emma, he shook out and lit a cigarette.

"I'll probably leave too in a couple of days," he said. "I have to go back to L.A."

Emma said nothing.

"I wonder," said David. "Everything here is so different from what I'm used to. I wonder how it would feel to run away like that—to risk everything to run."

Emma remained silent.

"You know, I think I'd like to write about that," said David. "I think I want to come with you. It'd be a killer piece. Western media would love that story."

Emma looked at David, slack-jawed. Her eyes narrowed in what looked like contempt.

"What is it with you and your articles?" she said. "I don't get your curiosity, David."

"Don't you see? To write about it I have to be there. I have to feel it!"

"Do you realize how ridiculous that sounds? You would put your life in jeopardy for a goddamned article!"

"I'm a U.S. citizen. They can't do anything to me . . . if I get caught."

"I'm sure that's going to make you bullet-proof in the dark," said Emma, "and the dogs will smell you're a U.S. citizen and leave you alone."

"Can you be a little more dramatic, please?" said David.

"Remember, David, they only check your papers after they kill you. And if they kill you, nobody will ever know."

She paced while David sat in the armchair, feeling squelched.

"Let me tell you something, Little Miss Hero," he said. "You've got your nice little flat here and stable little job no one can take from you. You want to leave all that, and you don't even know what you're up against. Nor do you even know what you'll find on the other side."

"Who do you think you are?" snapped Emma. "You don't have the right to judge me. You've no fucking idea. You mock what I'm trying to do. I'm doing this to fight for my life, not for a stupid article in a newspaper."

"Don't be naïve, Emma."

"Who's the naïve one? You want to create a situation so you can get a thrill and write about it." She paused. "You are disappointing, David."

"I don't get you," said David. "You've got your reasons and I've got mine. You make your way, and I'll make mine."

"Yes indeed," said Emma. "And where does that leave you and me?"

David looked at Emma thoughtfully. "What is it that you want from this—from you and me?"

"I don't know," she said. "I just know that I want more. I want to see you again someday."

"None of this makes any sense right now," said David.

He had to take his gaze away from her. The disappointment in her face was too much. He got up and began to walk around the room. "I can't make you any promises. I never could have anyway."

"I guess you're right," said Emma. "We can't decide anything. What is there to decide?"

"So—I guess this is it," said David.

WEDNESDAY, DECEMBER 6, 1989

Two days later, Emma paced around her apartment. She gazed at everything, trying to take in every detail. She was nervous, unsettled, feeling as if someone were watching her.

David, meanwhile, lay spread-eagled on his hotel-room bed, looking at the ceiling. He felt powerless as he went over every possible outcome in his mind.

The Guide was at home at his small kitchen table, eating a dinner of *galuste* soup.

Emma was in her bra. She was taping her papers and

money to her chest. She rolled the tape around her rib cage with precise movements.

The Guide was concealing a revolver at the small of his back. He had a duffel bag ready.

David put on jeans and boots and loaded film into the camera. He put his coat on and exited the room. Downstairs, he handed the key to the receptionist.

7:02 PM

"Will you be checking out, Mr. Martin?"

"No, I'm just taking a couple of days' trip to Transylvania. Please take my messages and keep my room intact." He had to do his best to deflect suspicion.

"We'll do that, Mr. Martin," the receptionist responded.

In front of the hotel, David found the Guide's waiting car and got in.

"Sorry. I'm trying to cover my tracks. Can't raise suspicions."

"Did you bring it?"

"Yes, it's here. All five thousand dollars. You can count it."

"It's okay. I trust you." A cash bribe had been enough to convince the Guide to add him to the party.

Emma put the icon she had tried to give David on the table. She looked at the face of Saint George, clasped her hands, and started to pray.

Bundled in warm clothes, Alex gazed out over the sea. It was a stormy winter evening. He was deep in thought, impervious to the cold and the wind.

7:24 PM

Emma was in her apartment, shoving a few more items into her luggage. Suddenly, she heard the elevator stop on the seventh floor and footsteps approaching her door.

She froze. The footsteps stopped.

The doorbell rang.

She panicked, pushing suitcase, purse, and clothing under her bed. She rushed to the door.

"Who is it?"

Silence.

"Who is it?" she asked again, looking through the peephole.

"State Security! Open up!"

Heart pumping, hands trembling, she opened the door slowly with the chain on.

A man of medium height and muscular build stood on her doorstep. She saw the militia uniform beneath his brown trench coat.

"What's the matter, comrade?" she asked in a low voice. "Can I help you?"

"Maybe. My name is Captain Popescu. I'm with the Department of State Security. Please let me in. I need to speak to Emma Grigo."

She unhooked the chain and opened the door wide. "That's me. Please come in."

The officer entered and took his hat off. His hair was short; he was balding, and his jaw line was well-defined. His complexion was dark, and he looked to be in his mid-fifties.

7:27 PM

"Please, step into the kitchen." She pointed in the direction of the kitchen, throwing a quick glance at the hallway clock. She was supposed to meet up with the Guide and David in less than thirty minutes.

She asked the officer if he would have tea. He assented. His boots were shiny, and his clothing reeked of tobacco. He sat at the kitchen table and looked around. Then he coughed and cleared his throat.

"So, Comrade Emma, what a beautiful career you have, hmm? A pity, really. You are good. You are good indeed. A renowned doctor and still so young. Young and beautiful.

"But now it could be cut short. It was brought to our attention that you've spent quite some time with two Americans lately. On Monday you didn't report for your shift at the hospital. You are a rare pearl of that institution. What type of relationship do you have with the Americans? Do have a seat."

She was in trouble. Someone at the hospital must have snitched on her.

"Please, Comrade Popescu," she said, turning her back to him while putting the kettle on. "On Monday, I took the day off." She turned on the flame to boil water for his tea. "There is no relationship with the Americans. "I'm just treating Alex Martin for some heart complications. That's all. I'm just his doctor."

"Never mind that. What do you have to tell us?"

"I have done nothing," said Emma. "I know nothing. Is this some kind of interrogation?"

"Leave that up to my interpretation. So, you have done nothing, and you know nothing. Do you think I came here for nothing? What, about Mr. Martin junior? David?"

"David is just visiting his father," she replied. She dropped a tea bag into a mug and poured, slopping boiling water over the counter. "He was worried sick about him." She placed the mug of tea in front of Popescu and took a seat opposite him at the kitchen table, her hands folded in front of her.

The silence stretched out, seeming to carve a physical space between the two of them. She was mortally afraid.

"Emma," said Popescu, "you know if you lie to me, you could face years in prison and we could revoke your license to practice medicine." He took a sip from the mug of tea, gazing directly into her eyes.

Hearing her name from his lips raised a lump in her throat. She felt drops of sweat on her forehead. She was blank for a second; then she looked back at him.

"I have no intention of lying to you. I'm telling you the truth. I met David for the first time less than a week ago."

"What kind of journalism does he do?"

"Hmmm, I wouldn't know. My understanding is that he is just starting out in journalism."

He looked at her, waiting, expectant. She could see the muscles flex in his jaw as he clenched his teeth.

She thought, she should have been prepared for this.

"How long is he here for?" asked Popescu.

"I don't know. I think a few weeks."

"Is that right?" Popescu took out a notepad and a pen. "Because I was just informed that he left for a trip to Transylvania. What is he doing there? With whom is he meeting?"

She felt dizzy. She chose her next words carefully.

"I do not know anything about his trip to Transylvania. I swear."

Popescu dropped the notepad, rose to his feet, and leaned forward, leaning on the table on clenched fists.

"I'm not sure you take me seriously. How is it you don't know anything about their doings and yet you spend so much time with them? Lying to a DSS officer is guaranteed imprisonment! You hear me!"

"I'm not lying to you." She glanced beyond him, at the clock in the hallway.

He turned his head to the clock and then looked back at her.

"Are we expecting someone tonight, Emma?"

She was in deep trouble. She needed to get rid of him quickly. He might wander into her bedroom.

"Well? Are we?"

"No, sir. I'm just tired."

"Tired from what? You haven't been at the hospital in a few days."

"I've been ill lately. It's the cold season."

He pulled out a pack of filter-less cigarettes and lit one up.

"I trust you don't mind," he sneered. "You don't look

like you're ready for bed. You look like you're going somewhere."

"No, I just got home. I was out doing a little Christmas shopping."

"Oh yeah, it is that time of the year. What did you buy and for whom?"

She could feel the blood pulsing in her neck, sweat rushing down her spine, and a sickening rush of adrenaline. She shook her head.

"Nothing, most of the stores were closed. Today is St. Nicholas Day."

"Ah. I don't see any boots by the front door. I guess St. Nicholas is not coming for you?"

Tears fell from her eyes. "I don't have anyone. My parents died a long time ago, and I have no family left in the city. I have an aunt in Bucharest, but we haven't been in touch in a while."

He raised his eyebrows at her. There was a long silence.

He looked again around the kitchen. Then he wandered into the living room. She stood and followed him.

"Comrade Emma," he said, "you claim you don't know David well. Let me jog your memory. Last Saturday, December 2nd, you were seen kissing him in the Casino restaurant in the old port. I think something is up."

He continued to look around the apartment.

"Our party leaders don't like traitors. They see the enemies of our state as arrogant. Enemies of Socialism. I can sense something is up. Something that could get me closer to retirement. It will help your career too if you tell me what's going on. Please recount what you did on December 2nd."

She could barely hear him. She was wondering if she could reach the front door before he could get hold of her. She couldn't remember whether or not she had locked it after he came in.

"So you are my commanding officer now?" she said. Then command me."

Popescu gave her a long look. She had covered half her face with her right hand.

"Miss, place your hands on your thighs and don't move an inch!"

She complied. There was silence.

"Tell me again what you did that day. What are the Americans up to? Whom are they meeting with? A false statement is perjury. You can save yourself. Don't forget what the State has done for you. It has given you your whole life, your whole little career."

8:41 PM

In the car, the Guide looked at his watch.

"Where is the doc?" he asked, his leg bouncing nervously.

"I don't know," said David. "I'm worried. Should we call her?"

"That's a bad idea, especially now. I'll walk over to her building and see if I notice anything. We need to get moving. It's getting late, and I don't like it. It's either now or never for your little friend."

He slowly got out of the car, looked left and right, and tucked his revolver in the back of his waistband. It was cold night in a deserted side street. The only noise was the distant barking of stray dogs.

David lit a cigarette. "If you're not back in fifteen minutes, I'll come after you," he whispered.

In the apartment, Emma was contemplating if she should make a run for it. Popescu strode back and forth. When he reached the other end of the living room, Emma pitched herself toward the entry door.

She had gotten as far as her hand on the door handle when she felt a hard blow to the back of her skull. The pain exploded. She crumpled to her knees. Popescu's fingers twisted in her hair. He grabbed a fistful and pulled, dragging her back into the kitchen. She wanted to scream, but the thought of alerting the neighbors stopped her.

In the kitchen, he let go of her hair and stood above her with one foot on either side of her hips. He bent down and put his hands around her throat.

"What's the rush, Comrade Emma?"

"Please let me go! I'm begging you. I have done nothing wrong."

"If you've done nothing wrong, why are you running?"

His face was an inch from hers. She closed her eyes. He bent to her ear and whispered.

"I have a proposition which you might find agreeable. Maybe both of us can find it so. Beneficial both for you and for State Security. Tonight everything could be over. You could go back to your element tomorrow. You could meet your patients. What do you say? Either go to prison, your career ruined, or cooperate with me."

He began to kiss her face and slipped a hand under her blouse. He had one hand around her neck, the other holding her breast.

"Please let me go, don't do this to me. Please!"

He took his hand from her neck and jammed it into the waistband of her jeans. He pulled her to a half-sitting position and dragged her toward her bedroom. She screamed, kicking, grabbing for anything she could.

Then came a loud crash, glass shattering. Popescu fell heavily onto Emma. She pushed him off. He was unconscious. She turned to see the Guide holding the bottom of a crystal vase.

"See what you made me do, Doc," he said calmly. "Now get your bags. We need to go!"

"Wait, what about him? We can't leave him here. Do you think he's alone?"

The Guide glanced out the kitchen window.

"Looks like he's parked in front. See—the unmarked black Dacia 1310. That must be his. We have a few hours before he wakes up. I'll take care of him. Go, please go. David is waiting for you in the car. It's a black Skoda."

The Guide hefted Popescu and carried him over his right shoulder out of the apartment.

9:15 PM

Emma rushed to get her things, her body shaking uncontrollably. She fished a diazepam from her purse and swallowed it. She felt nauseous, the pain in her head excruciating as she bumped along the floor. She knew she had no choice but to leave.

Emma stood in front of her building, looking up at her

windows. Her eyes swam with tears. She was about to embrace the unknown, to cross to the other side of the Iron Curtain. The air was cold in her lungs, the tips of her fingers blue. Her heart was filled with emotions.

She picked up her bags and walked towards the car.

"Jesus, Emma," said David, climbing out of the car, "what happened to you? Where is the Guide?"

"I'll explain when we get in the car."

THE ESCAPE

The Guide drove down a desolate country road. No one spoke. It was early morning hours, still dark. The car was small and cramped. David sat in back, Emma in front, holding an ice pack to the back of her head. The air was frigid—so cold it took your breath away.

They drove all night, westward towards the border with Hungary. After a while they abandoned the main arterial road. The Guide kept looking back to see if anyone was following. Finally, around dawn, he stopped the car on a dirt path.

"We need to get some sleep," said the Guide. "There is a safe house here."

"How far from the border are we?" asked David.

"About five kilometers. We'll walk there tonight." The

Guide paused. "If you want to change your mind, now's the time. Once we hit the forest, there's no coming back."

"I don't think I can sleep," said Emma.

"You'll have to," said the Guide.

They got out of the car and walked toward a house that looked abandoned. The yard was unpaved, the windows covered with dusty plywood. The wooden front steps creaked.

After a struggle, the Guide got the door open with a key. Inside, the air was dusty and dismal.

"The toilet is outside," said the Guide. "I'll go move the car to the barn." At the door, he turned around. "By the way, there's no electricity, heat, or hot water."

"Great," said David.

"I don't care," said Emma.

The Guide left them alone.

"You heard the guy," said Emma. "You still have time to change your mind."

"I know," said David. "I heard him loud and clear. But after what happened last night, there's no going back for me any more than there is for you."

"You are sick. Your curiosity is sick. You are playing with your life regardless."

"You're doing the same thing. Don't lecture me."

"At least I have a good reason."

"We all have our reasons."

"I'm sure you do."

Emma took her bags and disappeared into a hallway. David threw himself on a wooden bench, exasperated.

THURSDAY, DECEMBER 7, 1989

That night, three pairs of feet shod in heavy hiking boots trudged down a deserted country road. The frozen mud sparkled in the moonlight.

They walked single file. Once in a while, the Guide turned his head to check that the other two were still following. David was the last in line.

On the outskirts of a village, they heard the sound of fiddle music. They had reached a Gypsy camp. There was a large bonfire and three horse-drawn carriages. A group of Gypsies sat around the fire, among them several young people. A violin played a devilishly sly Gypsy song. A couple of women danced. They wore thick shawls, and their breath came out as mist in the frozen air, but still they moved to the rhythm.

The three were so close now that the Gypsies noticed them.

"Is it all right?" asked Emma, worried.

"Yes. Be calm," the Guide assured her. They kept

walking.

A Gypsy woman raised herself from the fire and walked toward them. Her fiery eyes were on the Guide. Coming closer, she made as if to touch him with the back of her hand and said something to him in her language. He listened gravely.

Then she stepped slowly, gracefully, toward David. The firelight was reflected in her eyes. She took David's hand and touched his palm with her fingertips. She said something, looked at him sharply, raised her arms at her sides, and began to laugh and dance to the music.

David watched in fascination. He pulled out his camera and took a couple of shots, but the Guide and Emma pressed him on.

Moments later, they were approaching the forest. It was dark and cold and had started to drizzle. Their faces were haggard. Emma shivered.

"I'm cold," she said. She turned to the Guide. "What did she say to you?"

The Guide had his head down, his hands in his pockets. "She said I'll marry the moon." He turned toward Emma as if he wanted to say something else. Then he looked up at the sky, at the moon. It was a full moon, perfectly round.

They kept walking.

"What did she tell him?" asked Emma, pointing to David.

"That he's got the breath of life on his skin but has lost the keys to his heart."

"Gibberish," said David.

"She's usually right," said the Guide.

The three of them lay in a field on their bellies, eyeing the border line. The moon, round and full, shone through the barbed wire of the fence, some fifty yards on. Everything was bathed in a sharp, silvery light.

"Do exactly as I do and stay behind me," said the Guide.

They got up and trudged through half-frozen watery mud. The Guide went on ahead, and at the fence, he crouched and began to cut the ground-level wires.

"On the other side of these wires is your freedom!" said the Guide looking at Emma.

"Hungary, then straight to Austria."

David and Emma sank to their bellies again and crawled through the deep mud. Slowly they advanced toward the fence.

As the moon slid behind a cloud, a shadow appeared on the ground.

"Wait, I see a car approaching. Stay low! It's a border

patrol car." said the Guide. The two companions were flat on the ground. Not moving.

"It will pass soon. Nothing to worry. They haven't spotted us."

"OK, clear. Let's go!" whispered the Guide.

Suddenly, David's boot hit the alarm wire. Sharp beams of high-wattage light cut through the dark. The alarm was louder than any sound they'd ever heard. Somewhere, dogs began to bark. Hurried steps shuffled in the frozen mud. The car they saw earlier started driving reckless in reverse.

A soldier—young-looking and surprised—appeared between David and Emma and the fence.

"Stop!" he cried.

Emma and David, on the ground, stayed motionless.

A platoon of soldiers came running from the right, answering the alarm. Three big, beautiful beasts of dogs ran alongside.

The young soldier had his gun raised. "Don't move or I'll shoot."

The Guide motioned to Emma and David to run. They scrambled up and started to run in the opposite direction from the platoon. The platoon leader yelled an order, and the soldiers released the dogs. Emma and David ran across the field in the dark, followed by the soldiers' flashlight beams.

The soldiers were screaming, running after the dogs. They were closing in.

Emma tripped and fell. David stopped and tried to pick her up.

"You gotta get up."

"My foot," said Emma.

"You gotta get up. I'll help you get up. We've gotta move." He pulled her hand from the mud. She was practically paralyzed with fear.

They looked back to see the soldiers and the dogs getting very close. The Guide had stopped.

David grabbed Emma, and together they ran toward the fence.

The Guide knew the young soldier would shoot him. All of a sudden his gruffness melted. He raised his head and looked at the stars.

The bullet left the barrel. The gunshot sounded. The Guide fell on his back. The last thing he saw was the full moon. Somewhere a Gypsy woman danced and laughed to the sound of trailing music.

Meanwhile, all Emma and David could hear was their breathing and the beating of their hearts. They began to climb the fence. The barbed wire ripped into the flesh of their hands.

David jumped to the other side. He passed no-man's-land and hid behind some bushes. He looked back to see Emma, stranded and at the end of her strength.

She was stuck on the fence. Her face was crushed against the wire. She'd been terrified, but now all the force seemed to go out of her. David watched in horror as the soldiers pulled her off the fence. She was caught.

"Oh, God," whispered David. He closed his eyes.

THE QUEST

The day before Christmas, David opened his eyes inside a cab in the old town in Constanta. He was bone-tired. He gazed outside the car's window to see people demonstrating in the streets. There were torn flags, tanks, soldiers, happy faces, candles, flowers. There were bonfires into which people were throwing books with red covers. The excitement was enormous. The entire country was literally up in arms—especially in Bucharest and Timisoara.

He had finally got his big break, but not the way he expected.

A WEEK EARLIER

He had been allowed to go back, and he had found his father. They were helpless; for days they didn't even know where she was and what had happened to her.

It had all started. A revolution, the break they had all been waiting for. He was happy for these people: happy and sad. There was so much innocence in them. He knew they knew nothing, nothing of what was to come. But he would write about them and their country. Communism had fallen, and he was in the thick of it. The luckiest break of his life.

Yes, he could write about everything he saw, everything he could hear and touch. But he couldn't write about what he felt. He couldn't write about her. He was too sad when he thought of her.

And for her, it was the biggest irony of all. If she had only waited a few days, everything could have been so much simpler.

As soon as he had seen her dragged off the fence by the soldiers, David had started running. He didn't know what else to do. He ran through that barren field, stumbling through brush and twigs, with no idea of direction. Somehow he held onto his backpack with his camera, but he had forgotten all about it. His brain seemed emptied of any thought. He was a mad animal chasing its tail in a wintered-over wheat field in Hungary until, finally, he collapsed from exhaustion.

He had run in a circle. When the farmer found him the

next afternoon—the sound of his tractor a somehow comforting mechanical whirring at the edges of David's consciousness—the fence would have still been just in sight across a quarter-mile of field. It was a spiky line on the horizon.

He spent three days in a Hungarian hospital. The furnishings were spare and the corridors dark, just like Alex's hospital back in Constanta, and there were many mornings when he started awake thinking he was back there. He thought he'd taken his father's place and that Emma was about to appear at his bedside in her white lab coat and stethoscope. He woke up thinking he could smell the ocean and hear the waves. But the rhythmic pounding would turn out to be nothing but the sound of a generator in the back courtyard.

He lay on his back, doubting he'd ever move again. He didn't know if she was alive or dead. He didn't know which he should hope for.

After he was discharged, his first visitor was a representative of the border patrol, a middle-aged man whose English was good enough to make genial conversation about David's travels.

"So what brings you to Hungary?" said the man, sitting on a metal chair next to David's bed.

"The truth?" said David.

"The truth, certainly," smiled the man.

"I was helping a friend of mine to escape Romania."

The man's cheerful, bland expression remained the same. He said nothing for several seconds. Then: "Helping, eh? In what way were you helping?"

"Well," said David, "I'm not sure. Perhaps helping isn't the word."

"Ah-hah," said the man and then waited some more.

"I just went along with her," said David. "I was worried for her, and I wanted to see what she would see. That's the best I can explain it."

The man gave his head a brisk shake as if waking himself up from a reverie. "You're known as a journalist. Perhaps you wanted to write a story?"

"Perhaps—yes," said David. "I wanted to write a story."

"Well," said the man, "that would indeed make a story! But your friend, then. Is she in Hungary now as well?"

"No. We got separated. I don't know where she is."

"Ah. And what will you do now? Return to the United States?"

"I'm not sure," said David. "Is that what has to happen?"

"Nothing has to happen, my boy. You may be granted

a short-term visa. We will welcome you, an American citizen, to stay in our country for a month."

And so David left the hospital, took the train to Budapest to procure the visa, and then returned to take up residence in a hostel in downtown Szeged, not far from where he had crossed the border.

The conditions didn't favor despair, although it would have been tempting to succumb. He had too much to do. He needed to contact his father. Alex hadn't know of David's plan, and indeed David had to acknowledge that it hadn't been fully complete. He had wanted to run with Emma. That was really all he knew. If they'd made it to the West, it would have been a fait accompli. Whatever Alex thought about it then would have been immaterial.

He'd placed her in more danger, but he couldn't think about that. He'd helped to get the Guide killed, but he couldn't think about that. He sweet-talked the desk girl at the hostel until she found him a local man who spoke good enough English to be hired by David to help him locate a phone number for Alex in Constanta. They tried the hospital first but never got an answer. They then tried to track down the family who had rented Alex his apartment. All David had for them was a street address. The Szeged local tried three different telephone operators with the address before he got a number that didn't immediately ring through to a recording. There was still no answer at it, but David resolved to keep trying it himself and released the Szeged man with five thousand forints and his thanks.

Emma, meanwhile, sat chained to the floor of a *Militia* van. The only other passenger was a bald older man, also chained at the wrists, who ignored her except for an occasional glance full of malevolence. Out of her mind as she was, she was almost intrigued by that. It was almost as if he knew her from somewhere. It was almost as if he personally blamed her for some great evil that had befallen him.

She must have fainted at some point. The next thing she would remember was sitting slumped in a chair, handcuffed to a table in an interrogation room. A man with a horrible face—mottled red and white, like a slab of fatty beef—was seated across from her. His head was cocked to one side as he sat quietly looking at her. His lips were pursed, which confused her, because it made his expression look as if he had just been asked a question and was considering how to respond. Wouldn't she be the one supposed to answer questions--? But she was sure she hadn't heard him ask one.

She would never be able to say how long she had sat

like that, across from him. She seemed to keep dipping in and out of consciousness. Like someone trying to stay awake, she would pull her head up and tell herself to focus, and she'd see the pursed red lips and start trying to think who had last said something, and then before she knew it she'd be wandering again, or maybe even outright dozing, before pulling up and starting the whole cycle again.

And then suddenly, "Comrade Emma!" a voice shouted at ear-splitting volume, and time started spinning again.

"Comrade Emma!" And the flat of a hand to the table, hard enough to make it shake though it was bolted to the floor.

"Comrade Emma! Sit up straight or you will be lashed to the chair!"

She did her best to comply.

And then, almost in a whisper: "Comrade Emma. Look me in the eyes when I speak to you."

She raised her head. Hair fell in her eyes. She longed to brush it back with a hand, but both her hands were cuffed.

She found herself trying to explain. "My hands—"

A sharp blow made the side of her head explode in stars. "Were you asked a question?" Another blow. "Speak! Were you?"

She managed to shake her head.

"Do you hear me! I have asked you to speak! Were you asked a question, before?"

Her confusion by now was complete. "No--?"

The whisper again. "That is correct. You will speak only when asked a question." The roar again: "Do you understand?"

"Yes—yes."

She was befuddled at first because it was the mottled-face speaking to her, and he never changed his position. He was always sitting directly across from her. She finally understood that he must have a henchman fetching the blows. But she never saw this person. He kept himself hidden, just beyond the periphery of her vision. Nevertheless, his timing was unerring.

She sat for hours—perhaps days. The room of course was a windowless cell. She sat until she pissed herself and then beyond that. The mottled-face man professed to be very disgusted.

"Comrade Emma! For the love of the motherland, sit up straight!"

She did her best to comply. And the first thing she saw was a familiar face, although she did not know at first why it was familiar. Her body knew it before her mind did, which was why she gagged. This, in turn, earned her another blow to the side of the head.

The face was Popescu's, the officer who had forced his way into her apartment. She recognized the square, bluff jaw. His head was bandaged. Below it, his eyes stared beadily at her. The beady eyes seemed out of place with the manly jaw. She shut her eyes so as not to have to look at him. Looking at him was going to make her gag.

"You recognize him, hey?" said her old friend the mottled-face man. "You know who this is. This is the comrade you lied to. This is the comrade who was beaten almost to death on your behalf. This is the comrade who knows exactly what a despicable slut you are."

She flinched for the blow, but it didn't come. The mottled-face man gave a snort of derision.

"Contemptible like all the others. All you enemies of the state are the same. You talk such noble ideals, but when the chips are down, you haven't got the bodily strength of a sick kitten. What kind of way is that to build a resistance?"

"You idiot, son of a bitch," snapped Emma. She had surprised herself with an actual emotion: anger. But she could never bear it when people made stupid assumptions about her. "You think I am an ideologue? You think I give a curse about a resistance movement? I am not trying to overthrow your precious state. It can reign a thousand years for all I care. I am doing no more than trying to release myself from it so that I can live free."

"Spoken like the decadent slut you are," said Popescu. Oh yes, he had to chime in. They had set him up in a chair to the right of the mottled-face man. "You care about no one but yourself and your filthy desires. About which we in Securitate know far too much, by the way. Your trysts with that American fool have all been captured on tape. You thought your apartment was some sort of safe haven—bug-free haven?"

"Really, comrade Popescu? You will pay for all of this! The tables are about to turn. Look at what's happening in Timisoara and the rest of the country. The regime is about to change. The entire nation wants this change, " said Emma shivering and sobbing.

Popescu approached her, put his face next to hers and spit on her face.

"You little bitch, we have evidence of what you did! I can kill you if I want to. At this moment, I am the regime!"

She would never, to her dying day, know if this was true. Probably, it was not. Interrogators lied routinely; this was basic knowledge. They could have surmised that David and she were lovers from the informant who had seen them kissing in the casino coat check. Still, the doubt would always somehow tinge with a tiny drop of poison her memories of her and David's affair.

But now, it only raised her ire. She would have killed them if she could. She had to stay quiet, though. She had already said too much. Not all of it was even what she believed. She didn't want the state to reign a thousand years. She wanted it to be ground to dust at this moment and reviled by the world. She would never, ever forgive them for stealing away her beautiful country.

The last thing they did was try to get her to admit that David and Alex were American spies.

"Why would that fool American insist on accompanying you when you tried to scuttle?"

"Because he wanted to write a story. He wanted to get an up-close, personal, eyewitness account of what it means to—"

"Of what it means to what?"

"To escape."

"To escape what?"

Of course she knew better than to proffer an answer, even if her silence did mean another blow, this one to the back of the head, where Popescu had struck her before. The pain made her keen and doubled her forward so her forehead touched her cuffed hands.

"You think we believe, stupid bitch, that the American

fool would run with you just to write a story?"

But she would say nothing more. And so they kicked the chair out from under her, and then they both stood up and upended the table, her hands still in the cuffs bolted to it. She fell forward over its upturned edge, spraining a wrist. And then they fell to. They kicked her in the head, the back, the ribs. It wasn't about interrogation anymore. They were avenging Popescu's humiliation, sure. And more than that: some larger anger that neither she, nor they, could have put into words.

Every day for three days, David went to the telephone office in the morning, the afternoon, and evening; paid at the cashier's counter; waited his turn; and attempted to place a call to Alex. He wasn't sure if he should give up, but the fact that the phone rang through, each time, gave him hope. The number wasn't disconnected. Finally, on the evening of the third day, a voice that sounded like an older woman's answered. "*Da?*"

"Alex—Alexander there?" asked David. The phrase exhausted most of his knowledge of Romanian.

"Alexandru? Da!" And then came a rush of more words.

When it stopped, he said quickly, in English, "He is my father. My father—my papa? Papa. I am trying to reach him."

"Papa! Da!" A torrent then of words—followed abruptly by a click. Had he heard the word for *goodbye* in there somewhere? He wasn't sure. But it was enough to encourage him to keep calling: the next morning, afternoon, and evening, and the next day after that. No answer, time after time. But there had been one once, so there would be again.

FRIDAY, DECEMBER 15, 1989

In the meantime, he moved like a ghost through his life, venturing out of the hostel only to visit the telephone office or to get his meals at the same small cafeteria. Out of the corner of his eye, he saw newspapers at newsstands, but he understood even fewer words of Hungarian than he did of Romanian. The desk girl had taken to smiling brilliantly at him; he nodded pleasantly back.

Then, on the afternoon of the fifth day, he reached his father. The phone was picked up, and it was Alex, answering as naturally as if he were at his own home.

"Dad?"

"David! Oh, my dear God. Where are you?"

"Dad, I'm so sorry—so sorry I couldn't tell you anything. I'm in Hungary. Szeged, Hungary."

David heard an intake of breath on the line. It sounded like his father was laughing. He did that: chuckled at moments of stress or confusion.

"Hungary, David. Hungary."

"That's right."

"And, pray, what are you doing there?"

"I don't know—honestly. Waiting, I guess. Dad—you need to know something. I came almost this far with Emma. She ran, Dad, just like you knew she was planning to, and in the end I couldn't let her go alone. She was . . . Dad, she was caught, and I don't know what happened to her next. I can't go anywhere until I find out."

There was a long silence on the line. Another apology was on the tip of David's tongue, but he bit it down. Let his dad come up with the next thing to say.

"David—what do you mean that you couldn't let her go alone? You are saying you ran with her and her Guide—you crossed the border with her?"

"I tried to—yes."

"How, *tried?*"

"We were stopped at the border. Soldiers and dogs. I cleared the fence, but she . . . Emma didn't make it."

"They caught her at the fence," said Alex.

"Yes."

"But you—you got away unharmed? How are you—

quite all right?"

"I'm all right now—yes. Shaken up at first, but functional now."

Another long silence passed. And then the chuckling started up. "David, David," said Alex. "Haven't I told you that you must find your own story? Talk about taking the opposite advice!"

"Dad," snapped David, "this is hardly the time for joking."

"I apologize," said Alex. "I wasn't meaning to joke. I am . . . stunned by what you've just told me. Well, we must arrange a way for you to come back to Romania. We need to find her!"

David couldn't help it; just as if he were a child again, he felt comforted by his father taking charge. "Dad," he said, "I just can't believe I finally reached you. It seems almost like a miracle that we're talking on the phone."

"It is a miracle, yes," said Alex in a serious tone. "You've been following the news?"

"No," said David, "I've not been following the news. I don't know a soul here and don't know a word of Hungarian."

"Well, then, I will tell you. Romania has erupted. In Bucharest and Timisoara, there is fighting in the streets. People are protesting against the regime. Hungarian language or no, I urge you to watch the next television you see. Something is happening here, David. You need to come back as soon as you can."

MONDAY, DECEMBER 18, 1989

He had returned to Romania by train, two days after that call to Alex. The borders were opened for a few hours. He could hardly believe he was going back, but he had encountered no trouble. His American passport seemed like a magic talisman now, just as he'd naively insisted it would be back when he and Emma were fighting about whether he should accompany her on her escape.

And then he was back in his hotel room—unbelievable how it had waited for him, so composedly, for almost two weeks—and meeting Alex the next day to try to find Emma. Alex had worked every connection he had at the hospital and the American embassy. And around them the whole time was swirling revolution.

The two of them bribed, bartered, begged. And just when they had given up hope, their efforts bore fruit. On David's third morning back, quite suddenly, he and Alex received a telegram notifying them blandly that Emma was being held in a state prison in a city called Arad, a ten-hour drive from Constanta.

There was a brief fight with his father. Alex told him it was folly to go after her, a folly almost on the same order as his initial one in insisting on accompanying her during her escape.

"But Dad, how can I do anything else?"

His father had relented after David had promised that he would spare no effort to phone him every day he was gone. And so David had set off that same day for the train station in Constanta and the next chapter in the story of his own personal revolution.

THURSDAY, DECEMBER 21, 1989

David had arrived in Arad late the next morning, after a noisy, sleepless night in the economy coach. His berth had been filled with drunken, card-playing men singing folk songs and spitting curses.

Ever since he had returned to Romania, it had seemed like carnival season to him. The scrim of decorum was gone from everyday society. Emotions ran high; strangers on the street were as likely to fall into each other's arms as to start a fistfight.

And Arad was something else again. Here was another crumbling, quaint city like Constanta (although without the smell of the sea on every street corner), lined with wedding-cake buildings and the winter air loud with car horns and televisions or radios playing in every storefront.

"What nationality are you?" cried the jolly matron behind the counter at the café where David had stopped, struggling with his phrasebook and dictionary.

"American," he told her.

"Wah—American, yes!" she bellowed and reached across the counter to slap him on the back, he assumed in a gesture of affection.

There was no phrase in his phrasebook for "I am trying to locate the state prison," but he did his best, rehearsing a likely-sounding sentence for use with the first cabbie who would listen. It took a few tries, but he finally found a cab driver who didn't shake his head and gesture David out of the cab after the first halting phrases.

This cabbie, a man about David's age with a military-looking crew cut, knew some English. "Prison!" he said. "What you want—you go to prison?"

David didn't know how much was advisable to try to explain. The language barrier might do enough of a job of censorship anyway.

"I am visiting a prisoner," he said.

The cabbie turned around to frankly stare at David. "You—a foreigner? You visit state prisoner?"

Now David thought for sure that he had said too much. But there was no going back. "I'm visiting a friend of mine—another foreigner—who is in the state prison or a military camp," he stammered.

The cabbie cocked an eyebrow and gave what looked like an exceedingly ironic half-smile. But at last he turned back to the wheel.

"Okay. I will take you to state prison," he said.

The prison was several miles outside the main part of town. It looked something like an old convent school, with a long limestone ledge behind the barbed-wire fence and a gatehouse underneath the arched entranceway.

David stopped at the gatehouse and spoke to the taciturn older man who sat inside it in a fur cap. He gave the man the contact name that had been in the telegram he had received about Emma's whereabouts.

"And I am here to see the prisoner Emma Grigo," he said. As he said her name, the rigors of the trip suddenly all fell away. Her name sounded so sweet in his mouth. She was alive! He was here to see her. Somewhere beyond that ledge, and through that other archway, and perhaps inside that long, flat building he could just glimpse in the distance, she sat in a cell, little knowing that he was but yards away.

"Emma Grigo," the man repeated, and suddenly David's heart fell. Her name didn't sound sweet on that man's lips; he mouthed it as if it had nettles. He said something else that David didn't understand, and then he picked up his phone and closed the sliding window through which he and David had been communicating.

David's time in both Romania and Hungary had accustomed him to watching people in offices hang on the phone for minutes on end, seeming for all the world to have forgotten he was there. He waited, not so much patiently as numbly. For the first time since he'd begun his journey, he felt the winter cold. The sharp air bit the tip of his nose.

The man was off the phone. He slid the window open with an abruptly scraping gesture. "Grigo!" he barked.

"Yes—Miss Grigo—where is she?" pressed David.

"Grigo! Not here!" There was more, but that was all David understood.

"Not here? Where--?"

David had his pocket dictionary in his hand. The man stood up and reached through the window, flapping his hand at it.

David handed it over, not without some misgivings. The man furiously flipped its pages. He found one and passed the book back to David, jabbing his finger at a spot.

David squinted to read the entry. A word in Romanian

and then the English equivalent, just to its right. *Released.*

"Yesterday," said the man, peering owlishly at David to make sure he understood.

"Released to where?" pressed David, desperately, but the man had slid the window to again and turned his back.

Back out on the main road, a cab pulled up alongside him. David looked in. It was the same cabbie who had brought him here.

"No entry? No friend?" said the cabbie, grinning.

"Just take me back to the train station," said David.

But in the couple of hours since he had first left the station, the atmosphere there had become still more chaotic. The cabbie could barely approach the station through the throng of people in the street, milling about and shouting in exuberance or anger—it was hard to tell. There were army vehicles all over the city. Young men with military uniforms taking pictures with civilians. David finally paid the cabbie the exorbitant amount he was requesting for his trouble and got out to thread through the crowd as best he could.

Inside the station, no one seemed to be on duty; people sat on the counters or moved about behind them with impunity. Finally, David was able to find a man in what appeared to be a conductor's uniform.

"Tickets?" he queried. "Where can I buy a ticket?"

"Where are you going?" barked the man.

"Constanta."

The man squinted and shrugged. David might as well have said he was going to Mars.

"Just get on the train!" said the man. At least, that was what David thought he said. David's Romanian had improved somewhat, even just in the time since he had returned from Hungary, but he still missed the great majority of what people said to or around him unless they spoke in short phrases.

The man repeated himself. "Just get on the train. When it comes. Pay on the train."

In the end, it took David two days to get back to Constanta, under regular circumstances a train journey of no more than twelve hours. But the things he saw and the people he spoke to on this journey, in a combination of his broken Romanian and their often-better English, formed the heart of the first major story he ever wrote as a journalist, a narrative of the Romanian revolution that he would sell to a well-known monthly magazine back in the United States and that would give American readers a taste of what it meant to be caught in the midst of a true revolution, with all its romance and violence and giddy hope.

Still, he greeted his first glimpse of Constanta, through a grimy train window just after dawn, with blessed relief. So many returns! It was almost like his hometown now.

Thinking of that reminded him of Alex, whom he realized with a pang he had barely remembered to try to phone. But he must find Emma first. He made his way through the station—more crowded than it had been before as well, but still more sedate than Arad had been; it was downright cavernous and echoing, by comparison—to see what he would find on the street.

He found low-grade chaos. Cars moved sluggishly through the roundabouts, blaring their horns. Barricades had been set up on several blocks. Televisions and radios played on every street corner here as well. Ceausescu had made his last, doomed speech from the steps of the Central Committee building the day before and was now on the run. His image was everywhere.

David decided to forego a cab. He'd had enough of relying on others to drive him through the welter of civil unrest. He'd trust his own feet. Emma's apartment was but a couple of miles from the train station.

His heart pounded as he rounded the corner to her block. There it was—her building, good old C1. She was alive. He allowed himself to bask in the relief of it all over again.

He reached the entranceway and found the buzzer with her last name. Of course, he didn't know if she'd be home. But he'd stand here all day if he had to.

It turned out to be only a minute. Above his head came the sound of a window sash flying up.

"Young man! For whom are you ringing?"

"I'm looking for Emma! Emma Grigo!"

"Not here! Not home! It is war here! There is massive shooting in the port. She is probably hospital!"

The quiet old hospital was like he had never seen it. No longer did it look semi-deserted, peacefully crumbling. Wounded people on stretchers lined the walls.

"Young man! Gangway!" He was standing in the way. There weren't enough beds! He made for the nearest exit, planning to gather his forces and make a plan for how to track her down. Suddenly, there she was at the top of a flight of steps from the loading dock. He runs towards her.

"David! My God!"

"Emma! You're here! You're working!"

"I'm not officially working, David." And indeed he saw

that she was in her regular street coat, not her white doctor scrubs. "I am only here because I had nowhere else to go just yet, and as you can see, they need all hands on board."

She was talking rapidly, her gaze darting nervously about. She wouldn't stop and just look at him, just raise that lovely face to him again with the eyes that seemed to shine forth her soul. That pure soul, pulsing alone and brave in a world of cruelty and calculation.

"David." Her fingers fluttered at his wrists, but still she wouldn't stop and look up at him. "What are you doing here, anyway? How is this any place for you? Even your father is no longer here."

"I know he's out of the hospital; he's been out weeks now."

"No, David, Alex isn't here in town at all anymore. He left days ago. I called at his friends' house, that family with whom he was staying."

"Dad left?"

"Yes! He saw he would be in danger here, and perhaps endangering others with his presence, so he caught a plane from Bucharest back to America, David. Where you should go now too."

"Emma—please." In his desperation he grabbed both her hands and held them tightly in his. She gasped, but now he had her attention; now she turned her face to his and looked at him. He saw fear and disgust in her eyes, but he felt nothing about that—not yet. The pain of that would be something he would feel later. For now, what he focused on was that her lip was cut and her face bruised. There was a black shadow around one of her eyes.

"Emma—in God's name. What happened to you?"

The hallway was noisy, with shouts and groans, so perhaps what he thought he heard he didn't really hear. But it sounded like she was growling, in her throat—like a hurt animal.

The next thing she said, he did hear distinctly.

"Let me go. Fool man, you let me go this instant or I will spit in your face."

He released her hands. She charged past him. He spun and watched her run down the corridor without another word.

Of course he couldn't give up. If he hadn't by then, he wasn't going to now. The next day he found that telegram with its contact name. It was a woman's name. He scoured through Emma's acquaintances until he found one who had good enough English and was willing to give him another clue to the identity behind this contact name. It was an older woman, an old friend of Emma's late parents. She had done well for herself, settling in a comfortable 19th century French chateau style house in the center of Constanta.

David had written her a telegram, saying only that he was a friend of Emma's and that he wanted to get her a message safely. Unexpectedly, she had phoned him right back. She was about to go away for a visit, she said. But she had given Emma the use of her house while she was gone. The poor girl needed a place to rest after all she had gone through. She would do anything for Emma. He writes the address on a piece of paper.

He grabbed a cab and gave the driver a note with the address: *Str. Grigore Tocilescu #24*. The driver was reluctant to take him to that part of town in Constanta. He notified David it's been a dangerous part of town in the past few days. The army was fighting Ceusescus' militia all over that neighborhood. They agreed on a price and drove off. He kept staring through the window. The commotion outside continued.

The cab slowly comes to a stop in front of a house #24. He was now in the old part of town in Constanta, where Emma was staying in the home of a friend who was away. The houses in this neighborhood were imposing, with large wooden gates framed by thick walls. The neighborhood looked like it had fallen straight out of the eighteenth century. People of all ages were chanting and waving Romanian flags with a hole in the middle. It was an euphoric moment.

David paid the driver and got out. He walked up to the house and knocked on the front door. No one answered. He knocked again.

Emma finally answered. When she opened the door and saw David, she had no reaction. She didn't even blink. Her face was bloodless, her eyes glazed. Her fatigue was the kind that doesn't go away with a good night's sleep.

"Come in," she said.

David followed her inside. The house was large and comfortable. Colored area rugs decorated hardwood floors, and the rooms were filled with old German stoves and heavy furniture. There were oil paintings on the walls and a gilded mirror.

Emma and David went into the living room. Books were everywhere.

"What are you doing here?" she asked.

"You didn't return my phone calls," he replied.

"I don't want to see you anymore," she said.

"Well, I came to say goodbye."

"So you're leaving."

"Yes. Alex says hi, too. He's already home. I had to stay a couple more days."

"Good then," said Emma.

David looked at her.

"What?" she said.

"Nothing," said David. "I was just thinking. Tomorrow is Christmas. I'd like to spend it with you."

"It doesn't matter," she said. "You can stay if you want."

"You're upset and tired and you're taking it out on me," complained David. "I thought you'd want to see me."

"I'm not upset," she said. "It was the roll of the dice. I'm leaving anyway."

David gave her a long look. Words seemed worthless.

"Why do you still want to leave?" he asked.

Emma spoke slowly, as if she had to force the words out. She seemed to contemplate what she was saying with sad eyes. David tried to understand the feeling betrayed in her look. It was neither fear nor regret. She looked, simply, spent with the effort of having to talk.

"It's not so hard to understand," she said, "and you already know it. What do you think is going to happen here, with all these changes going on? The smart and shrewd are going to stay on top; the others will get lost in the shuffle. It's going to be interesting and hard, but I'm too tired to want to deal with it." She paused. "I want to be free to live a nice calm life, David. It's all I ever wanted. I don't think I'll get it here.

"When they caught me, it was as if I suddenly woke up in unknown territory. Now my little world doesn't exist anymore. It's filled with muddy Army boots without leaving me any corner of my own. When they first caught me, I told myself everything was going to be all right once I could go back to my own dreams. But you know what, David? There is no going back. This is why I'm leaving.

"I'm tired. I'll show you to your room."

She turned her back and started walking down the hallway. David looked at her from behind. She shrugged her shoulders. The gesture found a way to his heart faster than any of the words she had just said.

That evening, Emma stood in front of the mirror. She was wrapped in a bed sheet, her hair wet. She searched her own face. Her lip was still cut and swollen, and she had deep circles under her eyes. The palms of her hands showed half-healed scars.

She sighed.

David, passing in the hallway, saw her bedroom door ajar. He saw Emma from behind, looking in the mirror. The sheet was hanging low on her hips though covering her breasts. On her back, he saw a large blue bruise in the shape of a boot print.

He pushed the door and opened it wider.

Emma saw David in the mirror and half-turned to look at him. She wrapped herself tighter in the bed sheet.

"What are you doing here?" she snapped. "Why don't you knock?"

"I'm—I'm sorry. I saw the door open. I saw . . . you looked hurt."

"It is none of your business, David," said Emma through clenched teeth.

He stared at her. "It *is* my business. I'm involved with you. I care about you. I want to know what happened to you. I want to know what I can do to help. Don't tell me I can't help."

"David, you are unbelievable," said Emma. She had begun to back away as he came further into the room. "You placed me in more danger by joining me and the Guide. You probably got the Guide killed. Have you ever thought about that?"

"Emma, you never understood," stammered David. "You thought I was only coming along for the adventure—to give myself a story. But that was just a cover—just bravado. Could you not see that? Couldn't you see that I couldn't have made any other choice? I was scared for you. I love you."

"Oh, David, David," said Emma. She sat down suddenly, heavily, on the dressing-table chair. "I even believe you. But can't you see it's far too late for talk of love."

"Why?"

"So much has happened," she said. "It can't make any difference."

"It doesn't need to make a difference. I don't expect it to make anything happen. I don't expect it to mean we can be together. I will never make any demands on you. Do you believe me?"

Emma sat silently for a long time, her forehead resting on her fist. She shivered a little in the cool air. Her body, in the bed sheet, was curled like a snail's. He knew he was causing her pain, and he wanted to leave, but he couldn't until she said just one more thing. It could be anything. He just needed to hear her say one last thing about her feelings.

"I believe you," she said finally, in a dull, flat voice. "I love you too. Leave me now, please. Get out of my room."

A table was set with a white tablecloth. Christmas carols were being sung. The table was set for two and laden with lit candles and platters of food.

David and Emma were sitting on the front stoop

listening to the carolers. Emma was wrapped in a blanket. David sat next to her, as close as he dared.

The carolers were men, dressed in national garb. They had hard, set faces. But they sang with pathos, expelling their breath in mists.

David felt abstracted, far away. Emma's face had more color, and her eyes were moist—whether from the cold or from the emotion of the carols, David couldn't tell.

He looked up. The sky was starry and clear. It had started to snow again. Moist flakes were falling from the sky. Far away, in Romania, an old way was being put to death and a new state struggling, in strife and hope, to be born.

———

NICHOLAS

At Phillip's party, Emma and David still sat by the fireplace, staring at each other. David's voice was calm and tired, but something in his tone had opened doors Emma had locked long ago. Behind those doors she had trapped the beauty of the feeling she had for him. She yearned now for what they had had. But whatever happened, those doors must stay closed.

"Back then," she said, "nothing was the way we wanted it. Life didn't give us what we wished for. We took what we could. Maybe . . . maybe I'd like those times to come back, but what for? I'm happy with my life. It's been interesting.

"I've just been back there, you know. I still have the apartment. It was my first time in ten years."

She remembered how she had struggled to open the door; after a decade, the lock was frozen. She had finally managed to unlock it and had stepped inside her old apartment.

What had it been like to see it again? Everything had been dusty and grimy. She walked slowly into the living room. Everything seemed smaller than she remembered.

She felt wondering, sorrowful. She walked through the hallway into the kitchen. It was grimy, just like the rest. And everything was just the way she had left it.

Something on the corner of the kitchen table caught her eye. She reached for it—the Ioannes Korais icon. As she picked it up, she looked at Saint George on the icon, and it almost seemed that he gazed back at her.

Something at the edge of the icon made her look more closely. She twisted it to the side. It was a piece of clear tape. She turned the icon over. It was a photograph.

As she studied it, emotions built inside her. Her lip trembled. She held a hand over her mouth to try to stop it. It was the picture Alex had taken of her and David on the beach. They were ten years younger and smiling happily for the camera. Emma could hear the waves breaking against the shore and the cries of the seagulls. The waters gently rolled.

Later, she had sat on one of the stone benches by the

sea. David was missing from the picture now.

The wine here, she reflected, was still sweet and tart and filled with bitter light. She had come back sadder and wiser. She knew she didn't have roots here, but she was still caught in a gnarl between the sea and the land.

———

Back at the party, David said, "Oh Emma, stop pretending." But then he saw Emma's eyes brighten and her lips curl into a smile. She was glowing. She was looking at someone or something that had appeared behind his chair.

David turned around to see Phillip holding the hand of a boy aged nine or ten.

"Look who wanted to come down and meet the guests," said Phillip. "He's a little sleepy—aren't you, buddy?"

The boy was sweet and innocent-looking. Also—as David saw and understood in an instant, before he could put it into words—he had David's eyes.

Phillip let go of the boy's hand, and he went to Emma. They hugged with fierce affection, Emma burying her head in the child's chest.

"Hi, Mom!" said the boy.

"Hi, baby! I'm so happy to see you. You always make me so happy, baby."

David stared at the child. He couldn't quite believe what he was seeing.

"I'll take him upstairs," said Phillip. "Come, Nick! Let's go."

Emma followed the boy with her eyes until he disappeared up the stairs.

"There isn't a corner in my soul that this little guy can't fill," she said.

David was thoughtful, contrite, confused. "How . . . how old is he?"

"Nicholas is nine years old," said Emma. She answered his unspoken question with a nod.

"How did you never tell me?"

"It would have been hard to tell you, David. I thought just maybe you would find out some time on your own. And now you have.

"And I've got something else that's yours," she went on. "But this one, I won't keep. I've decided to make it your Christmas gift." She reached down and brought up a package.

He took it and looked at her, saying nothing.

Outside, a car's horn honked.

"David, let's go!" said Alex waiting in the cab.

"Just a minute dad." he responded.

David looked into Emma's eyes for the last time.

Emma stood on the front stairs with Phillip's coat over her shoulders. David stood next to her, gazing down at her. There was the sound of carols. It had just started to snow.

"It's your cab," said Emma.

David walked slowly toward the taxi. He half-turned.

"I always think of you at Christmas," he said. Then he got in the cab and closed the door.

Emma watched it leave the driveway. "Goodbye, David," she said.

In the cab, Alex sat quietly, gazing out the window. David was quiet as well, holding the package in his lap.

Gingerly, he began to open it. It was the Saint George icon. He was shaken, not knowing whether to laugh or cry. He turned his face away.

He looked back at the icon and turned it over. There was nothing on its back anymore except a few traces of tape.

In her study, Emma looked at the photograph of her and David with a tender expression. She touched his face in the picture.

At the sound of Phillip's approach, she threw the picture in a desk drawer.

Phillip came in and seated himself on the sofa. Emma went to sit next to him. He looked at her tenderly.

"I think he really liked the boy," he said.

FACING REALITY

Two weeks later, a frazzled David was hurrying down Seventh Avenue in New York. It was midday, the sidewalk busy, the street full of honking cabs. He rushed into a grand building and into an elevator.

Sex. Love. Money. Hate. Fear. Loss. Pain. Change. All the right ingredients for the life he had chosen to live. And then he had found out he had a son. A son already half grown; he'd lost almost a decade of his life. He didn't know whether to be angry or glad. What was the right thing to do now? What was the *usual* thing?

For the past two weeks, he'd been working on an answer to that question as best he could. He had used the research tools at his disposal to find out more facts about when and where Nicholas was born and how Phillip had first come into Emma and Nicholas's lives.

He had found out that Nicholas was born in September 1990 in a hospital in Queens to Emma, who was unmarried. No father was listed on the birth certificate. Emma, at that time, had been working as a refugee counselor at a small nonprofit agency in New York City. Within a year, she had left that job and was working as an administrative assistant at a realty company. She had learned that business thoroughly, it appeared, moving up to larger companies until she had been hired as an executive assistant at the firm Phillip had founded when he was still in real estate.

David supposed he could push for a DNA test to confirm paternity. Anyone would have advised him to do that first thing. But he didn't need it. He knew. He'd seen the kid's face: his own face at that age. And anyway, the Emma he knew—and she still was the Emma he had known, despite everything—would not lie about something like that.

David already knew that Phillip and Emma had been married in the summer of 1994; he had seen the notice in the society pages of the New York *Times* when it had arrived at the offices of the L.A. paper that then employed him. In fact, it would have been difficult for him to forget that moment, the shock of it.

Up until then he had done a wonderful job, so he prided himself, of leaving Emma's memory in the past. He wouldn't say *forgetting her,* of course—but just tucking the memory away where it belonged. He had gone on with his own life—growing his reputation as a city journalist, dating women who had suitably similar backgrounds to his . . . although, of course, never really falling in love with any of them and never even approaching the consideration of marriage. (Usually, indeed, it was enough to mention once that he'd been down that road already; no more explanation was then required.)

Seeing her face in newsprint, staring up at him from the break-room table, was a fierce reality-check. She really had looked just the same in that picture as when he'd last seen her, four-and-a-half years earlier. Her hair had still been long. She'd been smiling, demurely, directly at the camera, with her groom, Phillip, by her side in quarter-profile.

That was his Emma all right, thought David, looking ahead while some man had eyes only for her. Only, now the man was Phillip Gordon, who, as far as David could tell, was well known strictly for being rich.

Well, after all, she'd said she wanted a nice life.

His recent research had suggested that it was a year or so after her marriage that she had first moved into the business of antiques dealing. He supposed he really shouldn't fault her for not remaining the idealistic doctor or the helper of refugees. She had done more to help others by the age of thirty than most people would or could have done in several lifetimes.

He shouldn't fault her. But he had always remembered her sharp summation—"David, you are disappointing." And he remembered how, staring at that wedding announcement, he couldn't help but whisper, "Emma, you are too."

And then, of course, six months ago now had come the recruiting phone call from Phillip's representative. Phillip was going in with some other wealthy men to found a new monthly magazine, and they wanted someone with journalistic name recognition to run the news department. It didn't matter that David had little to no magazine experience. At the time, he remembered, he hadn't dwelled on that discrepancy very long. The salary they were offering was double what he earned at the paper. He'd accepted the offer after brief negotiations and made the cross-country move in a spirit of adventure.

He couldn't help but wonder now about the possible ulterior motives behind the offer. Perhaps Emma was more involved with Phillip's business than either of them had let on. And perhaps she had been no less aware of

David's whereabouts, and his fortunes, than he had been of hers.

David came out of the elevator and walked briskly down the lavishly appointed corridor, past a panicked assistant. Her "Sir . . . sir? May I help you?" sounded in his ears. He pushed open the door to Emma's office.

Emma was on the phone, her back toward the door. She turned to see David planted squarely in front of her desk. He grabbed a chair and sat down uninvited.

"Something came up," said Emma into the phone. "I'll have to call you back in a few minutes."

"It's going to take more than a few minutes," said David.

"Well, hi, David!" cried Emma. "I won't pretend I'm surprised to see you."

"You know you wanted me to be here. Well, I'm here. Why did you never tell me? Give it to me straight."

"Things were always too complicated," said Emma.

"Too complicated? And then what happened? Now they're simple again? Emma, he's nine years old. He doesn't know me. At all. He doesn't even know I'm his father."

"Is it your big ego talking, or are you really concerned about him?" she fired back. "I never planned on *my son* meeting you like this. It just happened that way. I had thought about finding a way to tell you so many times, but then the time passed, and the longer I waited, the harder it seemed. Believe it or not, I didn't want you to meet him like this. I'm sorry it happened this way."

"Well, I want to be in his life," said David.

"All right. And how are you planning to do that?"

"Listen, Emma, I don't have a plan. But I want to be part of his life. I want to try. Please understand me."

"You should know something about him first," said Emma. "He's a great kid. He's very sensitive. He doesn't like cereal. He reads everything. He hates the smell of lavender."

David leaned forward, hands flat on the desk. "You see, this is a good start. But I want to find out things on my own." He leaned back. "All right—I guess we're in agreement. We'll work out the details. So I'll be seeing you. And I do mean that."

"There's one thing, though," said Emma. "He thinks Phillip is his father. I don't want you to ever tell him differently. I don't want you to mess him up." She got up and began pacing around the office. "Your curiosity can take you anywhere—you could suddenly disappear from his life and hurt him. Don't deny it. I don't want that to happen to him. You have to promise me you'll never tell him, and you must promise me you won't abandon him."

David reluctantly agreed. He made the promise.

It was Career Day, later that year, and David had been invited to Nicholas's school. He was to talk about where his journalism career had taken him. He looked out over the classroom crowd, all the eager little faces.

"My job is about stories," he said. "There are good stories everywhere; we just have to find them and help them come out into the world.

"My job takes me all over the globe. I travel to discover stories that I can write about. To do that, I have to be curious and ask myself many questions and keep my mind open to many ideas."

The children were mesmerized. Nicholas looked at David with sparkly, fascinated eyes.

He had met Nicholas one-on-one for the first time just a week after that meeting with Emma in her office. He had come over to the house on a Sunday afternoon for tea and been introduced as "Mom's dear old friend."

David had never been so nervous in his life. He was afraid he might babble, or move his arm and break a vase by mistake, but as soon as he saw Emma come in holding Nicholas by the hand, he relaxed. Nicholas seemed so open, sweet, and smart. Practically the first thing he did was ask David if he wanted to see his toys, and when David said yes, he whipped out a thingamajig like a Rubik's Cube made of small metal marbles.

"It's called a Buckyball!" said Nicholas. "Dad gave it to me for Christmas. It's cool!" He showed David how it worked, how the balls were magnetized and you had to figure out how you could use the magnets to bend it into various shapes. David didn't even have time to wince at the sound of Nicholas calling Phillip *Dad*. Later, they played with a regular Rubik's Cube, and David pretended he had seen the whole *Star Wars* franchise, resolving inwardly to rent all the videos and make sure he was up to speed by the next visit. Ditto for the Harry Potter books.

"That was fun!" said Nicholas shyly at the end of the visit as David stood putting on his coat. Spontaneously, he grabbed both of David's hands in his and whirled with him a moment. "I'll play my records for you next time and we can dance!" he said.

"He really liked you," murmured Emma, squeezing David's forearms as he stood in the doorway. "We will do this again. Everyone is happy about it. Phillip too."

And so they had done it again. At least every other weekend unless he was traveling for work, David would visit, and Emma would tell him every time how excited Nick had been ahead of the visit, counting the hours till

David would arrive. Pretty soon, David and Nicholas began to take field trips of their own, going to museums, movies, ball games. Nicholas had as many passions as David did, and they shared them all.

There were times, though, when in spite of himself David fell into what Nicholas called his "dark-face look." It wasn't always easy for David, watching Emma, Phillip, and Nicholas making up a family unit and himself on the outside, playing the role of hip uncle or trusted family friend.

"What's your dad like?" he asked Nicholas once, early on, trying to sound casual. "Do you do things together? Play catch in the yard?"

Nicholas gave him a funny, smirking look, just as if he knew what the edge in David's voice meant. "Catch? No. I don't know. Maybe."

If Phillip ever came in when David was with Nicholas, David watched them intently, alert for any sign that Nicholas treated Phillip with special formality or distance. Nicholas was such a serious child anyway, though, that David had to admit it was impossible to measure.

As the years passed, David would gradually stop comparing himself to Phillip; he would come to accept the relationship as it stood. He would even delight in getting under Nicholas's skin from time to time. It was wonderful that Nicholas would trust him enough to sometimes grow annoyed with him. When Nicholas turned thirteen, fourteen, David asked the inevitable question—"Any girls you like?"—and secretly enjoyed Nicholas's eye-rolling.

Right from the start, Nicholas showed all his writing to David. David watched as the carefully printed letters on lined paper became neatly word-processed manuscripts. Nicholas begged David to give in-depth critiques, and David obliged. Nicholas devoured all his comments, although he also wasn't shy about making it clear when he didn't agree with them.

"David, you're telling me it's all about the story, but this is a case when the facts trump the story."

"No, Nicholas, you're wrong. One never trumps the other. The facts *are* the story. You have to write so that the reader never questions one or the other."

"The *story*, the *story*," grumbled Nicholas, and David was pleasantly shocked to hear in his voice a reminder of Emma's exasperated, "You would risk your life for a story" from fifteen years before.

When David stood in front of that Career Day class, the events of 9/11 were still more than a year in the future. Nicholas would turn eleven just before that day; there would have been a birthday dinner for two of Nicholas's closest friends, his parents, and David at Four Seasons. Nicholas, Emma confided, wasn't one for huge parties. Then, three days later would come 9/11, and for David no effect of it was more important than the fact that he could not see Nicholas for days afterward. David, marooned in Manhattan, might as well have been on the other end of the world.

But finally, one day, after two long weeks, came the phone call from Emma: "Nicholas is dying to see you. We all are." He had taken the train out to Bedford; Emma and Nicholas had come to meet him at the station. He had embraced each of them tightly. 9/11 had meant that he could feel Emma in his arms again, even if only for a moment.

Nicholas had been in a grave mood, drawing quietly while David sat reading. He made no direct reference to current events except to ask David, at one point, whether he thought the country would now go to war.

David had said he thought so. "What do you think of war?" he asked Nicholas.

"I don't like war," said Nicholas. "It just leads to more war."

"You don't think it solves problems, eh?" said David.

Nicholas shook his head.

"But if countries couldn't go to war, wouldn't other

bad countries be able to take them over?"

'Not if there were no guns or bombs," said Nicholas.

"You may have a point there."

"When I grow up," said Nicholas, "I want to write stories that will show people why war is wrong. I want to show all the people it hurts."

"That's a wonderful ambition," said David and then bit his tongue. He had almost added, "*son.*"

But all of that was still to come. Now, David looked out over the assemblage of fifth-grade children, letting his gaze be pulled over and over to Nicholas's bright stare.

David was giving the kids the "big talk"—his regular spiel, watered down. But he couldn't tell them that the greatest gift this career had brought him was his son. It was something David would have to keep to himself: how much he wanted to be there for Nicholas, to guide him and protect him.

He loved him.

"Some of you might become engineers," said David, "some of you will be doctors, and some of you will be lawyers. But there must be at least one person here who will become a journalist, who will want to travel the world and experience its daily miracles.

And when that happens, I can't wait to read whatever you write." The class filled with joy and laughter.

THE BITTER TRUTH

On an early morning fifteen years later almost to the day, David sat strapped in his seat in a C-130 military airplane about to fly from the U.S. Air Force base in Ramadi, Iraq to Munich, Germany.

He had been in Iraq four months now and was ready to head home. He was wondering if this time really might be his last in Iraq. Every time he left, he assumed he'd never be back—sometimes promised himself he'd never be back—and of course he'd been wrong every time.

What drew him back was usually a personal appeal. Someone he'd befriended needed his help, or else he wanted to check in again with someone he'd been writing about—a family or one of the many everyday heroes he profiled, doctors and aid workers and the menschy street vendors who helped rebuild the neighborhood after bomb attacks. The people he worked with and wrote about, he couldn't put out of his mind when he returned to the United States. His life in Iraq might seem like a dream to him then, but it was one he dreamed every day.

And then after a while the dream would start to seem more real than the daily American life around him. He couldn't tolerate a quiet life for very long. Nine years he had walled himself up in that gilded cage of a magazine in New York: that had been enough quiet, padded, trivial luxury to last him the rest of his life.

He'd had a taste of mortal danger on that winter night in 1989 on the Romanian - Hungarian border fence. He wondered if it was an addiction and if it had started then.

If so, then the Islamic State was his pusher. Since the rise of ISIL, David had traveled as an embedded journalist with three different regiments. He'd been at close range in raids; he'd seen up close what people called the fog of war. He'd seen soldiers who'd been friends of his killed; he'd gone through something of what the soldiers went through when a comrade fell. He knew people—colleagues—at home who took a dim view of embedded journalism. He knew they thought of it as playing at war.

Maybe they were right in a way. It was a little like a

game. Maybe he was addicted, sure. But he felt a sense of mission here he'd never known before. The people he wrote about here—the soldiers, the Iraqi civilians—needed the world to know their stories.

"Where're you headed?" he asked the reporter next to him, a bluff, crew-cut fellow about David's age with piercing blue eyes.

"Dallas, Texas. How about you?"

"New York. I'll be home in twelve hours! I'm already two days late. Didn't get the clearance to fly back until this evening. My son is going to hate me. He's graduating from journalism school as we speak."

"Aw, he'll understand," the other reporter said.

"I hope so," said David.

It wasn't the first time he'd referred to Nicholas as his son when talking to someone who'd likely never meet the boy. His lips twitched now with the desire to keep talking—to tell this friendly colleague all about it, exactly what it meant for him to call Nicholas his son.

"You go to journalism school yourself?" asked the man.

"I didn't," said David. "College degree in English and then working up from small-town papers. The old-fashioned way."

"You said it," said the man.

"My boy is getting his graduate degree from Columbia," said David.

"Hot damn! That's a great school. You must be proud of him," said the man, beaming back at him.

"Extremely proud of him. I'm the happiest dad on the planet," responded David, with a smile on his face.

"Y'll get to congratulate him in no time. I'm sure he'll understand the circumstances for you being a little late," said the Texan.

06:10 PM, NEW YORK CITY

In New York, a young man stood at a dais, receiving an award for the most outstanding graduate work in the most prestigious journalism program in the country. He was being recognized for his master's-thesis project, an expose of fraud in a chain of agencies catering to low-income renters that had first been published by a neighborhood weekly paper and then been picked up, with further reporting, by the New York *Times*.

"Thank you so much," said Nicholas, smiling brilliantly. "I still can't believe I'm standing here in front of all you amazing people to receive recognition for something I love doing. Every one of you deserves to be standing here as well."

He made an expansive gesture toward the audience, where a middle-aged Emma beamed with pride. As Nicholas spoke, he searched for David, but all he saw was an empty seat.

"I have had wonderful professors and brilliant fellow students," he went on. "But I wouldn't be here at all if it weren't for the person who helped me the most, the person whose professional advice I relied on first and last, the person who since I was a little kid has never failed to make time to listen to me and answer all my questions. That person is my friend and mentor, Mr. David Martin.

"All those years he encouraged me to pursue the impossible, and he believed in me when it felt like no one else did. I am the person I am today because of our family friend David Martin.

"His reputation preceded him everywhere. I know he has a reputation for being cutting and sharp, but he is also one of the wittiest, best-hearted people I've ever met.

"What I learned from him is that nothing can be achieved without a risk—and no one can grow as a person if they haven't put themselves on the line."

01:25 AM, RAMADI, IRAQ

The transport plane was taxiing for takeoff. Besides David and the reporter from Dallas, it held twenty or so currently snoozing troops. The night sky was clear. It was a full moon, and the plane seemed to be racing directly into blackness at the horizon.

David was suddenly overcome by a strange feeling. He felt pierced with a sense of absurdity and beauty, a more poignant sensation than anything he'd felt since those chilly gray winter afternoons in Constanta, that city seemingly outside of time, twenty-five years before.

The sweet and the tart cancel each other out, she had said. *What's left is bitter light.*

Was that the name of the feeling he was having now?

How strange life was! Here he was, fifty years old and younger inside than he'd ever been, secret father to a grown son, a macho reporter in military fatigues surrounded by sleeping soldiers, careening into a desert in a country called the birthplace of civilization. And no one to whom he'd ever been close in this wide world had the ghost of a notion where he was at this moment.

The wind whistled in his ears. The plane was airborne. Tears stood on the rims of David's eyes.

06:30 PM

To heavy applause, Nicholas walked off the dais, award in hand. Everyone seemed to want to shake his hand and pat him on the back.

He smiled as hard as he could, trying to fight down the misgivings that filled his heart. Emma could spot those sad eyes on his happy face. *After all, it wasn't a given David would be here.* He and David had emailed about it; Nicholas had known it would be touch-and-go as to whether or not David showed up. There was the clearance to get and then the military transport plane, with its frequent delays, to rely on. There was the possibility of bureaucratic red tape at beginning, middle, and end of the journey.

He hadn't expected to feel devastated if David was a no-show.

01:32 AM, SOMEWHERE NEAR RAMADI, IRAQ

Suddenly, the right side of the plane erupted in an explosion. David went blind for a second, his ears ringing. The night sky lit up over the desert. Smoke and fire filled the cargo hold. He could hear the pilot yelling.

"Mayday, Mayday. This is Charlie 130-5. We've been hit. I repeat, we've been hit. Lost engine one, losing pressure."

The plane went through a cloud buildup. Another low-altitude alert sounded.

"We're going down!" the co-pilot exclaimed.

Over the radio came the voice of the approach controller. "Charlie 130-5, do you see Ramadi USAB on your left? You're clear for emergency landing."

"We can't! We're losing it!" cried the co-pilot.

" C-130 heavy," said the approach controller, "reduce speed to one-seventy. You're coming in way too fast. Turn left two-seventy."

The gear warning horn sounded. The left engine was overheating. *Whoop, whoop,* came the noise of the ground proximity warning system.

"Pull up, pull up," cried the pilot, frantically trying to get altitude.

"Oh God, we're going down," said the co-pilot. "We're going to crash."

A few minutes later, at the crash site, two medical helicopters had arrived for rescue.

"Any survivors yet?"

"Negative. It looks really bad. God damn it, we need fire engines here ASAP!"

"Roger that! Requesting assistance.."

"The main fuselage is unrecognizable. I hope we get to identify the bodies."

"Create a safe perimeter. There is debris splattered everywhere!"

"Roger that…"

"I have the passenger manifest. Over…"

"How many on board?"

"Fifteen passengers. Two of them are civilians and eight USAF crew. Over…"

"God Damn it! It's a black day for us."

"You have permission to notify DOD and SD immediately! Casualties are high. Chance of surviving this explosion is almost inexistent. Most likely total loss."

"Roger that!"

"Good Lord! This entire plane was obliterated! May these souls rest in peace!"

07:15 PM

"Beautiful job of the speech," his dean was saying. She pulled him in for a quick embrace. "We would love to have David Martin teach a guest course next time he's in New York. There's the writer-in-residence position. Give him the good word?"

Nicholas smiled and squeezed her arm. He felt enveloped by well-wishers. Where was his mother? He gazed, a little wildly, over people's shoulders. Toward the back of the room, he saw Emma with her phone to her ear. She was hunched over, looking down. He couldn't read her expression.

With one last bright, abstracted smile, Nicholas broke

free of the crowd. He wove through the chairs and tables, keeping his eyes on his mother. She stood now with her phone in her hand dangling by her side, staring at the ground.

Nicholas had a terrible feeling. He stopped for a moment, holding to the back of a chair with a white-knuckled hand.

"Mother?"

"What is going on?"

"What is wrong?"

She didn't appear to have heard him. She moved forward now with a tottering motion, reaching out for the nearest chair. Her jerky gesture sent it to the floor. She bent, slowly, and righted it. Then she lowered herself into it.

Nicholas guessed the worst from her movements alone. His graceful, nimble mother. He had never seen her move like an old woman.

He went to her. She lifted her pale face to meet his. He sank to his knees and hugged her legs, head in her lap.

Emma moaned softly, cradling Nicholas's head in her hands..

Nicholas heard her and suddenly understood something. Her hurt was beyond his own pain.

Holding tightly to his mother as she mourned, he

understood that David was much more than a dear friend to Emma. And in some deep way he realized the rest of it as well.

"David is gone!"

"What do you mean, he's gone?" asked Nicholas.

"DOD just phoned me. The plane David was on crushed next to Ramadi."

"Oh my Gosh, that's terrible! How could this...? I'm so sorry mom!"

"How can this be possible? Dad died, now David... What is happening to us? Why is God punishing us?"

"Are you sure about this? I mean, are they certain of this?"

"Yes, complete annihilation! They were probably shot down by the rebels in Iraq."

Nicholas puts his arms around Emma. He holds her tight.

"I'm so sorry mom! I'm so sorry..."

"You, David, you always left me at the worst of times," keened Emma.

But she knew that in truth, David had never broken his promise not to abandon Nicholas. She knew that David had hated his job at Phillip's glossy monthly magazine, but he had kept it for almost nine years—right up until Nicholas entered college. Then, liberated, David had quit to become the freelance journalist he had perhaps always been meant to be. Hearkening back to his adventure in Romania almost twenty-five years before, he had refashioned himself as a war reporter and decamped for Iraq, Afghanistan, Syria. Nicholas, meanwhile, was attending college in New York City, and whenever David was home, the two were together constantly. They would come to visit the house and stay up half the night together in the living room, drinking, bouncing ideas off each other, arguing, laughing.

The day of David's funeral was rainy and cold. The funeral was closed-casket. Alex, Emma, and Nicholas sat beside each other, and after the service, Emma walked to the rim of the burial site and dropped in a picture.

It was the snapshot that she had taped to the back of the Ioannes Korais icon. It landed on the coffin to be battered by the rain.

"I thought it was hard when I lost Phillip," she said. She turned to Alex and buried her face in his chest.

Later, people were walking toward their cars. When Emma got to hers, she turned to Nicholas and looked at him with loving eyes.

"You understand, right?" she said. "You understand why I didn't tell you? You forgive me?"

Nicholas caught her hands in both of his. "There is nothing you need to be forgiven for, Mother," he said.

After Phillip died suddenly of a heart attack when Nicholas was a senior in college, she had called David and Nicholas *her menfolk*, and she had come to rely on the bond between the two of them, more than ever.

A few years before, with his inheritance from Phillip's estate, Nicholas had bought a house by the beach, where he stayed as often as he could on breaks from the city. It was a small, pretty Arts and Crafts bungalow, a piquant contrast with his youth. It was simply furnished, comfortable in the way of a writer's retreat.

One mild June evening, he sat at his desk there. He had been drinking. Indeed, since David had died, he had been drinking quite a bit. While David was alive, he had never pursued David's alcohol hobby as avidly as David had, but now that he was dead, he drank not only in tribute but somehow to keep David alive.

That, at any rate, was what he told his friends, the closest of whom were still leaving worried voicemail messages every other day. He hadn't crashed any cars into telephone poles yet, but he'd been near-catatonic at one or two parties and had closed a couple of bars by himself, insisting that his friends should go home and that he was fine.

David's death was worse than Phillip's because Nicholas hadn't known what he was losing, in David, until after it was gone.

And he couldn't even really be angry about that. Oh, he had tried it on for size, being angry at David and Emma for keeping secrets, but the truth was that it was as he had had told Emma: there was nothing she needed to be forgiven for. He was a grownup who had had a few romances of his own. He knew how complicated things could get. And that was even before taking a revolution into account.

All the same, he'd been robbed. David should have lived another thirty years—forty years. Nicholas was sure that if David had lived, he would have told him sooner or later that they were father and son. The chances that had been lost, the feelings Nicholas had no place for—all of them drove him to drink.

It had been enough to worry Emma, she who had spent so much time in the company of those world-class drinkers, David and Phillip. But with her trademark grace and common sense, she had held back from lecturing, or scolding, or begging him to grieve differently. She had only told him, please be careful.

Or maybe she had been too deep in grief herself to try to correct his way of doing it. How many long, sad weekends had there been with just the two of them at her house? He had a paid internship at the *Times* starting later that summer but until then, nothing to structure his time. He had originally planned on a long camping trip out West with several friends to celebrate the end of their studies, but he'd cancelled his part in this and had retreated into mourning.

Emma, for her part, was busy with her business during the work-week, but as soon as Friday evening came, he would go to meet her at her office, and the two of them would ride the train home together, sometimes tightly holding hands the whole way. Back at the house in Bedford, they would pick distractedly at the meals the cook had made ahead and wrapped for them, and then they would sit side by side in easy chairs in the living room, assuring each other every hour that in just a few more minutes, they'd rouse themselves and go to bed.

The truth was that they couldn't bear to be out of each other's company for any longer than absolutely necessary. More than once, they slept on the couch and lounger in the living room, under blankets Emma found in the hallway closet, rather than part into separate bedrooms for the night.

She had done right, Nicholas thought now, in not fretting him. During the past few days, he felt he had turned a corner.

He looked around him, this June evening at a cottage on the beach in East Hampton, NY. The lights were dim, and he was surrounded by stacks of paperwork. But for the first time in more than a month, he felt at peace.

In his hand he held a large Manila envelope, addressed to him in David's script. It held a letter that David had written several years ago, on the occasion of his first reporting trip to Iraq. Nicholas had read it several times before this evening—in numbness, in confusion, in anger, in sorrow.

Tonight he opened it again. He found something new in it every time he read it. Tonight, in his newly quiet mood, perhaps he'd find himself open to receiving everything it had to say: its unspoken message as well as its spoken one.

My dearest Nicholas—

If you're reading this, it means I'm not around anymore. I know the risks I'm taking, and I did not want to leave without telling you some things it's important for you to know.

I have had a good life. I didn't set out to make a fortune, but I haven't done so shabby either. Everything I have is yours, because as long as you walk the earth—well, you'll be my son.

I'm not speaking in parables here. I met Emma, your mother, when we were both too young to know yet what we were about. Later, when you came into my life, I was afraid you'd hate me for abandoning you. But I want you to know that I loved you since I found out you existed.

I hope you're not angry with me, although of course you have a right to be, because I never told you the truth. I did promise your mother that I would not. But then, later, I could have broken the promise. Only, the longer I waited, the harder it became.

Nicholas stopped to sip from his glass of Jack Daniel's whiskey and to look at the sun setting through the window.

You are my son, Nicholas, and I am so proud of you. Please think of me sometimes. Life has always been interesting for me, and I don't know if that's a curse or a blessing. I always thought that my writing would be my legacy—that I would be remembered for my sharply etched stories and my clever turns of phrase—but the truth of the matter is, people will forget me. It's in the nature of things.

But you, Nicholas, because you are my child you will always carry me with you, and I will always be a little part of you.

You were the best hand life ever dealt me. You are my ace in the hole, the light of my life, my son.

Nicholas put the paper down on his cluttered desk, where the Ioannes Korais icon was bathed in the soft light of dusk. Outside, the beach was empty, the waves sparkling in the dying light. As he lifted his eyes from the letter, he glanced at his mother, who was sitting by the window with a faraway look on her face. Now middle-aged, she still looked beautiful.

Words did not pass between them. They did not need to. Nicholas and Emma had always communicated most powerfully without words, and that was truer than ever now.

For David was in the room with them. They both felt his presence, as they listened to the seagulls' cries and the slapping of the waves against the dock. They both felt that if they turned their heads, they would see him in the corner, curled up in his armchair by lamplight, notepad in lap, writing. And they each imagined how he, feeling their gazes on him, would look up, his face relaxing into his mysterious grin. As they each squinted at the unshaded window, they could almost see his reflection in the darkening glass.

They were a family, reunited, and that would never change.

———

END